THE FIRETONGUE HEIR

ELYSE THOMSON

TWO LAURELS PRESS

The Firetongue Heir

Ebook ISBN: 978-1-7388426-6-7

Paperback ISBN: 978-1-7388426-7-4

CONTENT WARNINGS

For my readers who prefer not to read the content warnings, please feel free to skip this section and dive right in.

For my readers who would prefer a list of content warnings before proceeding, I've provided what I hope to be a fairly substantive list below.

Content Warnings: Domestic violence/abuse, child abuse (historic), death, blood and gore, maiming, swearing, sexism, classism, animal death, consensual on-page sex.

GLOSSARY

King/Queen: Ruler of one of the kingdoms of Lethe (Arcadia, Kolkhis, Eleusis, Pontos, Temenos, Apollonia, Aeolia). Often co-rules with the heir to the throne. Addressed as Your Majesty.

Crown Prince/Crown Princess: Heir to the throne. Addressed as Your Royal Highness.

Prince/Princess: Child of the king and queen. Addressed as Your Highness.

Prince Consort/Princess Consort: Fiancé(e) or spouse of a prince/princess. Addressed as Your Radiance.

Noble Titles in Descending order of Rank

Illustrus: Male landowning nobleman with a significant estate and/or distinguished military service. No stylized form of address. Plural = Illustri

Illustra: Usually, the wife of an illustrus. Rarely, a landowning noblewoman with a significant estate and/or distinguished military service. No stylized form of address. Plural = Illustrae

Nobilissimus: Son of an illustrus or a minor nobleman with a small estate. No stylized form of address. Plural = Nobilissimi

Nobilissima: Usually, the daughter of an illustrus or wife of a nobilissimus. Rarely, a minor noblewoman with a small estate. No stylized form of address. Plural = Nobilissimae

<u>Military Titles</u>

Strategos: A general of a kingdom's military forces. Answers to the royal family directly.

<u>Slang</u>

Elemental: A mage with an elemental magical gift (water, fire, earth, air, light or darkness). Elemental gifts comprise the vast majority of mage gifts within Lethe, and are expected in all those of royal birth.

Elementalist: Elemental magic elitists who discriminate against those without elemental magical gifts (control of fire, water, earth, wind, lightning, darkness or light). They believe theirs is the superior form of magic.

Menial: A derogatory term for a mage without an elemental magical gift.

Feral: A derogatory term for beast mages.

Ignoble: A noble born without the expected elemental gift of their family bloodline.

LETHE, THE LAND OF MAGES

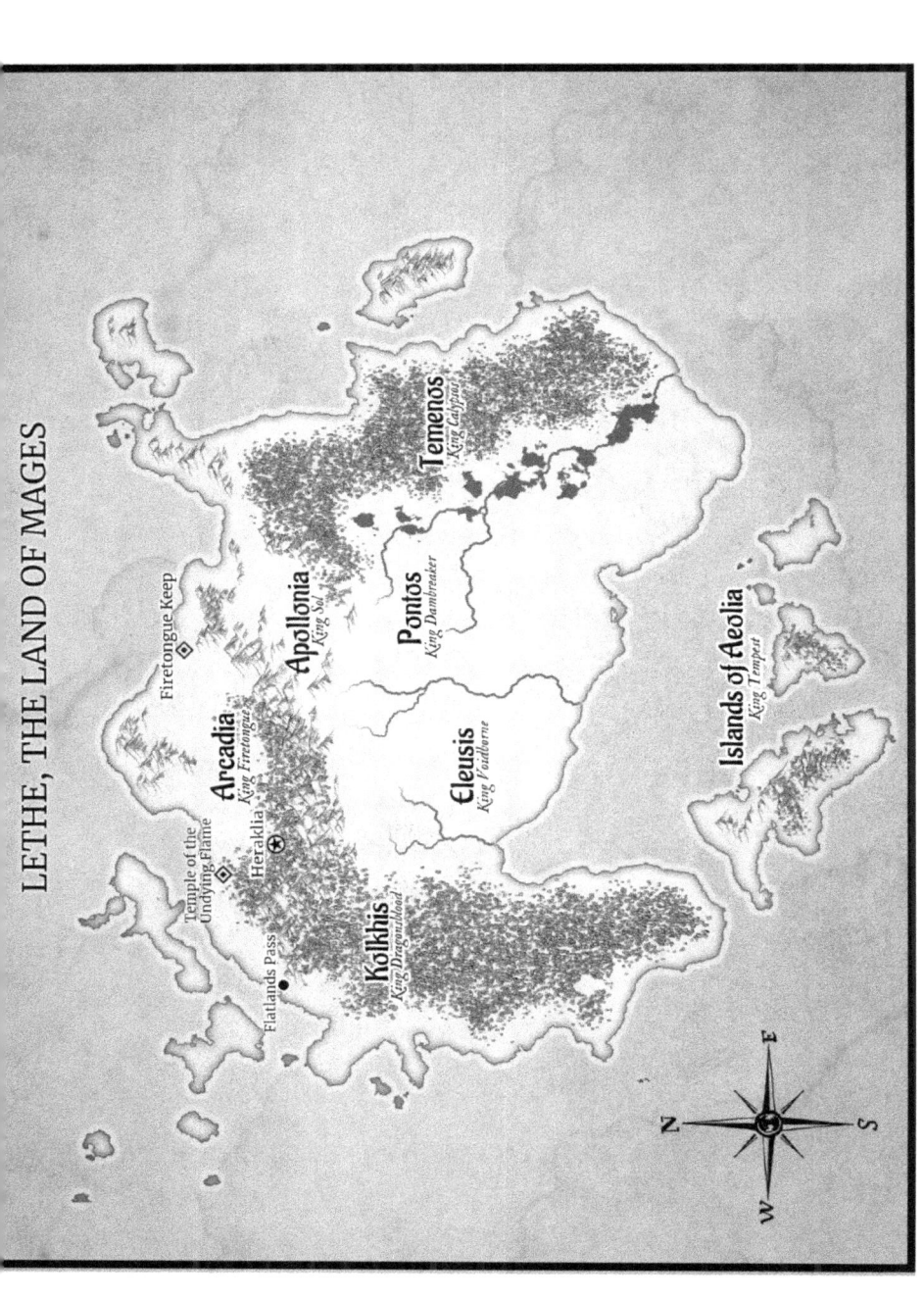

To everyone who has championed my words,
This story is my gift to you.

CHAPTER 1

Darius was not a well-loved prince.

Being the youngest son of a despised tyrant, and the one responsible for the unenviable task of recruiting nobles for the war effort, meant few were willing to do more than respectfully get out of his way. It was why, though he stood between the ever-popular garum and spiced meat vendors, the spit and hiss of oil crackling all the while, every would-be patron had given him a wide berth. It also came as no surprise, as he leaned against the wall between the shops to tease the most beautiful woman in the city of Heraklia, that he was met with neither fawning nor flattery.

"You're nothing but a brawler, a reprobate and a flirt. I'll have nothing to do with you!"

Darius couldn't help his grin. It opened the cut on his lower lip, which probably only proved Nadia's point. At times like this, when he could see her fighting to keep her lips from quirking, her eyes alight, he felt like he'd won the greatest prize in the land.

"But you like it when I flirt."

Nadia's withering glare had felled lesser men. She looked down her long nose at him, pursing full lips, her hazel eyes darkening the longer their stalemate lasted. The mask she wore was impressive, but just that—a mask. Reaching out his hand, his calloused fingertips glided across her fawn-coloured cheeks as they heated. He tucked an errant strand of impossibly soft jet hair behind her ear and leaned in.

"Besides, no one loves arguing with you as much as I do," he whispered.

The late afternoon sun blazed in the sky and the market street was a cacophony of colour and smells. At least near the food vendors, the aromas were pleasant. It was the perfect place to spend an hour in the company of the woman he most cherished while he avoided his royal duties.

Male groaning interrupted the moment. Darius curled his lip at the man just now staggering to his feet and climbing out of the cobbled roadway, where he had been holding up a produce-laden wagon. Traffic resumed, though passersby still gave the trio a wide berth.

Nadia leaned out of his touch, eyes mutinous but her cheeks blushing wildly.

"Come along Phokas, I'm certain His Highness has other people to harass."

"He started it," Darius muttered.

"You attacked me!" Phokas fumed, brushing dirt from his fine green robes and tunic.

"You tripped over your fancy boots trying to get in the first swing." Darius rolled his eyes.

"Because you were trying to seduce my sister!"

At least Nadia's irritating elder brother was right about one thing.

That two siblings could share so many of the same features while inspiring two such opposing feelings was a marvel. Only a shade above average height, both wore their long, black hair partially in elaborate braids, the rest falling down their backs. Nadia also wore fine, embroidered silks, a gown of beautiful turquoise and simple gold jewelry. One day, maybe she would wear the jewellery he would buy for her.

Unlike her brother, she was not a nattering fool.

He supposed next to them, in his dusty military leathers fresh from forcing a new sad group of young men into his father's army, he looked exactly like the kind of ruffian Nadia thought him. His short beard a few days out from a proper trim, thick dark hair scraped back from his face in a messy pinned braid and the grime coating his terra-cotta complexion was probably not helping his cause. Still, he couldn't help tweaking their noses.

"I wasn't trying, Phokas. I was succeeding." He winked at Nadia.

She huffed indignantly and turned away, though the tips of her ears were pink.

"She is engaged, you mangy bastard! And to a man far better than you could ever dream of being. Persist in your delusions and I shall complain to King Barziya himself!"

Nadia's shoulders stiffened.

Well, there went his mood. Darius bit back a curse.

"Phokas, don't. Please. We'll be late if we stay any longer." Nadia touched her brother's hand and smiled, placating him. No one could resist her smile.

"Oh, yes, I suppose you're right." He patted her hand, giving her a wan smile. Then he turned back to Darius, a sneer on his face. "My sister will always be too good for the likes of you, prince or not."

Darius' only use was as breeding stock for his father's precious elemental gift, one never to be squandered consorting with those whose bloodlines were tainted with anything but elemental magics. Families like Nadia's. In truth, Phokas had the right of it. Darius could promise her nothing, his future forever held in his father's iron fist, and the whole kingdom of Arcadia knew it.

"Careful, Phokas, or I'll be a good little prince and recruit you for the war like I'm supposed to."

That had the obnoxious man skittering off, dragging away the only good thing in the whole kingdom of Arcardia, probably in the whole of the continent of Lethe, too. He waited, watching as they left.

Look back, Nadia.

She turned her head, catching one last glimpse of him before they vanished around the nearest street corner. His heart leapt.

Success.

Even having to drag today's sorry recruits back to King Barziya's temporary residence couldn't dampen his spirits. At least, that's what he'd thought. As soon as he'd done so and gone to clean up after a long day, he was summoned to the king's presence. It was an event that never boded well.

Darius strode down crowded palace halls bustling with harried servants and grim-faced noblemen. Scuffed, dusty mosaics decorated the floors while dirty, chipped frescoes coated the walls. There was no coin for the upkeep of such things, not with a war on and a king in residence. And King Barziya Firetongue was using his time here as much to muster a fighting force as to beggar the owner of the palace, Illustrus Heraklius Lithos, a man who had, decades ago, insulted Barziya before he'd claimed the crown of Arcadia. Never one to let a petty grudge die, Barziya was gleefully enjoying his revenge. By the time they left for Firetongue Keep in the East, the people of Heraklia's palace would be well and truly bankrupt. Darius had long thought his family was more akin to a plague of locusts than anything else, and his father's actions had never dissuaded him from the notion.

His seventeen half-brothers were already in the columned main hall, skylights painting every surface in a rosy glow as the sun set. Thick columns held up a frescoed roof, the walls done in the same faded red as the pillars, painted green rose vines the only colour to break up the monotonous hue. His brothers' faces, so much like his own, were grim as they nodded along to whatever tirade Father was on. Good little princes, strategoi in their military regalia always ready to do whatever cruel, foolish things Father demanded of them, rising up the ranks of His Majesty's esteem. It was exactly as Father preferred it, refusing to name an heir lest the rest of his sons stopped desperately trying to please him. Even

Mardonius, the eldest, had been forced to grovel and jump for Father's favour. Unlike Darius, who was perpetually a thorn in his father's side.

"-and you!" Barziya howled, pointing a bejeweled finger at Darius.

The king's red eyes glinted with fury as spittle flew, his long white hair flapping like a cloak around his shoulders. Barziya's stomping strides ate up the distance between them, no doubt adding to the damage to the rose vine mosaics under his feet. Though he was getting on in years, his tawny complexion heavily lined, the king was by no means frail. Age hadn't softened a single thing about him, except perhaps his grip on his temper.

Pain exploded in Darius' left eye.

He'd seen the punch coming, but dodging it would have only made things worse. At least he would have one to match the bruise on the right side.

As a boy, Darius had been convinced he would gain his father's love if only he could stop angering him. As a man of nearly thirty, he now understood there had never been any love to gain. The violence had always been a given. How else was his father to shape him into a man exactly like himself? Once Darius had accepted that, he'd managed to harden himself against his boyish fantasies, and instead held to the determination that he would never become like his father.

"You worthless," A blow to his gut left him winded and falling to his knees. *Shouldn't have taken off the armor.* "lazy," a blast of fire stung the skin of his exposed arm, "unfilial," a kick to his side stopped just short of breaking a rib, "whore's get!" Barziya spat at him. "You think I don't know about you sniffing after that jumped-up farmer? You think I'd let you breed with some inferior *menial*? With *my* blood coursing through your veins?! You belong to me, boy. Your life is *mine*! Be grateful I haven't sent you to the deepest of hells, the same as your bitch mother."

Rage burned in Darius' chest. No matter how often Barziya slandered his late mother, Darius' emotions were little more than dry kindling to the spark of that insult. He knew he should swallow his words, refuse to give his father the reaction he sought, deny him one more spurious reason to beat him—but he couldn't. Mother had been the only one to have ever loved him. And Barziya had killed her for the temerity of protecting him from being beaten.

"My mother was a paragon! *You* were unworthy of *her*!"

It seemed he'd be spending the evening in the dungeons after all. Voice wheezy and pained from his beating, Darius had dared to bark back. He would never apologise for this, never regret protecting her memory. And he would never forgive this man for killing her.

The room was still, frozen in shocked silence. No one insulted King Firetongue and lived. Darius could see him contemplating filicide, the satisfaction it would give him to see the thorn in his side finally gone for good. But even the King had limits. A dead son was a terrible waste, especially when there were alliances to be made.

Barziya had only killed one of his children, the son who had been the people's favourite, the one his enemies had attempted to replace him with. Not one of his remaining sons had ever attempted to curry favour with those not slavishly devoted to the king ever again. Despite his being the obvious black sheep of his father's home, no one had the stomach to approach Darius with a similar scheme in mind—not after what Father had done to the previous traitors.

Barziya gripped Darius' face in his hand, a punishing hold that dragged him up from his prone position on the floor.

"Your mother was a frigid bitch. Vain, stupid and greedy. I did the world a favour when I wrung her ungrateful neck." Barziya gripped Darius' neck and squeezed. "My tolerance has limits." Darius glared, daring him to squeeze harder. It wouldn't be the first time Father had choked him out. Barziya obliged. Darius struggled. But it was not the lack of air that concerned Darius. The satisfied gleam in Barziya's eyes sent a shiver of fear down his spine. "But maybe you're too thick-headed to be taught with beatings." Barziya tossed him to the ground. "Datis, go out and find that menial bitch. Have her whipped and cut up her face. Let everyone know it's because she dared covet my blood."

No. Not Nadia!

Darius lunged, ignoring the pain, and tackled his father to the ground. Grabbing the knife at his father's belt, he was inches away from severing an artery when he was dragged off by five of his brothers.

For a brief moment, his father had known fear. Then it was gone. He shoved aside anyone fool enough to try to help the old king to his feet. Barziya's slow laugh sent ice directly to Darius' heart.

He'd erred.

Bile crept up Darius' throat.

"It seems I've finally found the right incentive for you, boy." Barziya's smile was triumphant. "Send him to the dungeons. Bring the bitch to me."

CHAPTER 2

Nadia's mind was elsewhere as she toyed with the miniature painted soldier in her hand. Prince Darius Firetongue was the bane of her existence. He made her want things she couldn't have, with his easy smiles and casual touches, his sparkling ruby eyes and his quick wit. She was promised to another, an alliance her family required if they were to survive the war on their doorstep. Banishing the annoyingly charming rogue from her mind, she set the soldier back down on the map before her, golden rays of the setting sun burnishing the leather to a warm hue.

The Great War had dragged on, it's sixth anniversary just next month. So far, the kingdom of Arcadia had survived mostly unscathed, its long southern border protected by the mountains. In the East, Firetongue Keep protected its short, vulnerable border with the warring kingdom of Apollonia. But here in the West? The kingdom of Kolkhis had been harrying the border towns where the mountains tapered off. Ostensibly allies, Kolkhis and Arcadia had a long history of cooperation. But King Dragonsblood was busy trying to conquer his other neighbours in the war engulfing Lethe, leaving the border with Arcadia vulnerable to banditry and unscrupulous strategoi emboldened by their king's greed and inattentiveness.

If Nadia didn't marry, her family, situated in the Flatlands Pass, and all the people who depended on them for protection, would inevitably succumb to the chaos currently consuming Lethe. Few were as committed to stability as those whose lives and bloodlines straddled both sides of the border between the kingdoms, and few were as vulnerable to hostilities. They'd spent the last six months in the city of Heraklia, away from home, for the very purpose of marriage negotiations. She supposed it was her good luck that both heads of the families made mules blush with their legendary stubbornness. The Bladesworne family was famed for their berserkers, while hers, the Verdants, were famed for their bountiful harvests—thanks to plant magic mage gifts like hers. Her family's wealth, their family's prestige and raw power—it was a good match. A strategic match given the threat her family faced. One she'd helped see to fruition.

Nadia ran a finger along the border of the map.

But that was before Darius.

A man she could not have. A man whose father was a virulent elementalist, no matter that gifts like hers kept people fed.

"Nadia darling? It's almost time."

Nadia blinked, dragged out of her reverie by her brother's voice. Phokas was her favourite brother, not only because he was endlessly kind to her, but also because he knew her skills and respected her for them. The oldest of eight siblings, Phokas would one day be the head of the Verdant family, and likely her greatest ally.

If only the other men of her family, or any of those of her fiancé's, would see her worth. If only her own mother could.

"Of course." Nadia straightened. "Illustrus Bladesworne already sent the best of his fighters to the Flatlands ahead of King Barziya's visit." It had been a bit of timely advice which had won Phokas the Bladesworne family's gratitude and respect. One of many triumphs, she hoped. "Firetongue won't chance getting so close to the border, even if he is hard up on finding more of his meat-shields. They should remain undiscovered so long as they stay hidden. The king will depart within the month, once Illustrus Lithos has run out of coin to entertain him. Our spies in Kolkhis say Strategos Illyia isn't especially well-loved by King Dragonsblood. Right now, he busies himself raiding villages along the main road. There has been no indication that he plans to deviate from it when he get to the Flatlands. I propose we set up an ambush here." Nadia moved the soldier. "Before they arrive, we'll evacuate the town and burn the buildings. King Dragonsblood will be too busy to send people to check our claims that they aggressed first, not when our messengers bring tales of what his strategos has done to his own people."

"How will we ensure none of their soldiers escape to spread another tale?" Phokas asked.

"We curse the town."

Phokas grimaced.

"That will require a lot of gold."

It would, more than they could afford. Which was why Nadia had not been idle these past six months in Heraklia. Instead, she'd made alliances with many a curse mage, among others.

"Letting them into the Flatlands proper or allowing their soldiers to escape will cost us a great deal more."

Phokas seemed unconvinced.

"If this goes our way, our family secures an alliance with King Dragonsblood himself. The only thing he loves more than his bloodline is useful, competent people. You could be wed to one of his daughters or nieces before the changing of the seasons. That, more than my marriage, will protect our lands from the depredations of this gods-forsaken war."

Kolkhis was one of the largest kingdoms in Lethe. Having its alliance would also be the first step in her long-term plan. If she could steer her family down the right path, then the tyrant Firetongue's days would be numbered.

"As usual, you're right. Run through the scheme once more. Hopefully the heads of our families will heed your words."

Her words, but spoken with Phokas' voice. It had always been thus. Nadia was the one who'd helped bring bountiful harvests, a role suitable for a woman like her. A role her mother had long instilled in her. Strategy and plotting were the preserve of men. She prayed to remain in Phokas' company long enough to see her family through this next great hurdle. Only time would tell if her new husband could be made malleable. Berserkers, what the Bladesworne family was known for, rarely were, given the uncompromising mental fortitude it took for them to withstand the darker aspects of their mage gift.

If she had to replace them later, then so be it. It was another worry for another day.

Once Phokas was confident he could recite her plan without issue and answer questions the heads of their families might ask, Nadia retired to the garden. It was a small, peaceful space in the Bladesworne home, one oft neglected, save by the gardeners. Vibrant green filled the space, along with a myriad of colourful, fragrant blooms. All around were tall red columns and clean white and black mosaic floors. Passing by the attendant, Nadia smiled and handed the woman a salve, the rare, costly ingredients created with the aid of her magic.

"For your grandmother."

"May the forgotten gods see fit to remember you, Nobilissima." The woman smiled back. "Enjoy your respite."

"You have my gratitude."

Nadia looked around, ensuring she was truly unwatched, before she sighed. She could claim no great power for herself, save the alliances she'd created with those who had even less power than she. Servants were often ignored, expected to be neither seen, nor heard, yet always useful and always at hand. In her six months here in Heraklia, she'd used her mage gift and her smile to win over the whole Bladesworne household staff, and infiltrate every other household in the city. Servants carrying letters and doing errands had become her scouts; those who dusted and swept her gossips; those who cooked and shopped her eyes and ears. And at times like these, they knew she wanted time alone and ensured she had it.

She should be in her assigned room, embroidering her wedding dress, but she couldn't, not today. Another lecture from her mother would undoubtedly await her once she heard that Darius had spoken with her. 'Marriage is not about love' was the refrain most often spoken these days. Another favourite of Mother's was 'men like that are beasts.' It was followed closely by 'love leads to a woman's ruination.' No, she had no desire to embroider or listen to the same lectures she'd heard every day since she was old enough to know what marriage was. Nadia was as likely to stitch a picture of Darius' face into the cloth as she was to do anything else. Seated under the shade of the fig tree she closed her eyes.

The rogue had made a habit of slipping into her fiancé's walled home under cover of darkness. Once he found her, he would needle her without shame, fearless of the consequences of being caught. Or they would simply discuss their days, gossiping about the townsfolk as if they were an old married couple. Free from the need to don her proper, public mask, she could enjoy trading barbs with him. Most of the time though, she treated his never-ending cuts and bruises with her salves. Darius used every treatment as a way to seduce her—tucking her hair behind her ear, skating his fingers across her knuckles, every caress a brand on her heart.

But he was forbidden. And Nadia had long ago learned to harden her heart. There would be no love in her marriage, just as there was no love between her own parents. Not that she loved Darius. And not that she had allowed herself such girlish fantasies.

"Nadia!"

Startled, she nearly fell off her bench. Heaving himself over the wall of the garden with stiff movements was none other than Darius.

"You can't be here. Not now. Not in broad daylight!" She hissed back at him, frantically scanning the area for others. It wasn't precisely broad daylight, with the sun beginning to set, but it was much too bright out nonetheless.

"You must come with me Nadia. My father, he—"

"Nadia!" Phokas shouted, rushing towards her, his face ashen. He dragged her behind him the second his eyes alighted on Darius, a blade of ice in his hand. Phokas was no match for Darius, despite his elemental gift.

"Phokas, don't!" Nadia cried.

"He's here on his father's orders to drag you back to King Firetongue on spurious charges. They're threatening to maim you, Nadia. Stay behind me!"

"Do I look like I came on my father's order?!" Darius hissed, cradling his side. His left eye was nearly swollen shut and a weeping burn crept up his arm. The king had beaten him. Again.

"One of your brothers is beating down the door as we speak!"

"Oh gods." Nadia swallowed. All her plans would be for naught if she were maimed. Illustrus Bladesworne would reject her family's proposal, while the Verdant family reputation would be destroyed. King Firetongue's ire would brand her family as pariahs.

"Nadia, we can escape out the servant's entrance. Come." Phokas tugged on her, a wary eye on Darius.

"You won't make it more than a block without being caught. Datis has the exits covered." Darius held out his hand. "Please, Nadia, you know I would never betray you to my father."

Phokas stepped between them, snarling.

"She knows nothing of the sort!"

"Phokas, stop." Nadia pulled away. If her plans were less than useless now, then the only thing she could do now was to protect Phokas—and her family. "I'll give myself up."

A chorus of vehement no's met her pronouncement. She couldn't believe she had to argue in favour of her own maiming. Bile crept up her throat.

"If I flee with you, you'll be killed, Phokas. We all will. You must protect our family."

He gripped her hand in his, shaking his head.

"I don't care! I won't let him hurt you!" Phokas' face reddened with rage.

Tears stung her eyes. She placed her hands on his cheeks. She would protect her brother, no matter the cost. He'd done right by her all her life. She owed him this at least. Phokas was in high dudgeon now, but he knew as well as she that he had no real martial skill.

"But he might not kill anyone if I'm the one to abduct you." Darius broke the melancholy spell. "It will have to be ugly, though."

Phokas and Darius shared a look of understanding.

"No, what are you thinking?" Nadia's heart raced.

"Swear on your miserable life that you'll protect her, no matter the cost," Phokas replied, his countenance grave as he stepped away from Nadia.

"Phokas, no!" Nadia tried to grip her brother's robes, but Darius caught her up, wrapping an arm around her waist, pinning her at his side.

"You have my word." Darius nodded.

"You cannot do this without my consent!" Nadia shrieked.

"Make it look like a real fight, Firetongue."

Darius nodded, launching a wall of flame at Phokas. Nadia's screams merged with her brother's. He launched another at the soldiers bursting into the garden.

"Nadia, if we're going to survive, we must flee!"

"Phokas, he—"

"Honour his wishes or his agony will have been for nothing!" Darius shouted as he launched another molten wave at the king's soldiers.

Nadia nodded, heartbroken, and allowed Darius to drag her over the garden wall.

CHAPTER 3

Darius had fought like a man possessed until he was subdued by his brothers Tithaeus and Datis. They hauled him, beaten, broken and burned, to the dungeons, past the beast mage guard, Dihya, before tossing him into a dingy cell, a sprinkling of urine-soaked hay the only padding against the rough-hewn rock. Rancid oil lit the few flickering lamps in this neglected hovel. It stank of rot and piss, the frigid rock quickly leeching away any bodily warmth.

If he had only a single broken rib, it would be a minor miracle. As his brothers turned the key in the lock and marched off, Darius counted his hurts, trying to find a way to stand. He had to stand.

He had to warn Nadia.

"Pissed off your old man again?"

Darius groaned as he turned to his less-injured side, refusing to take the bait. The silver-tongue mage had the only cell with a proper bed and a few sparse amenities. Had he been less of a violent, wily bastard, the silver-tongue might have been allowed to live in the palace above. But then again, probably not. Anytime he managed to slip his collar, the only thing that could keep his magic in check, he had the power to bring even kings to their knees with only a few words.

"You know, I could take care of that particular problem for you...if you took off my collar."

Yes, the mage would solve all his problems, for however long it took to then turn on Darius himself. The man's sole use was in interrogation.

Only a fool would risk more than that. And though Barziya coveted some of the rarer mage gifts like that of the silver-tongue or the teleportation mage he kept on hand, they were simply that in the king's eyes—useful tools that were not to be fully trusted.

Darius got to his hands and knees, breath hissing through clenched teeth as blood poured from one of his many cuts into his eyes. Gods below, he was a mess.

"Get back, Miltiades! Fucking silver-tongue scum." The beast mage guard Dihya sneered.

Miltiades, rattled the bars of his cell.

"Says the jumped-up animal! Fuck you, Dihya! Gods damned feral!" He spat.

She deftly dodged the man's spittle.

"Animal? Can't come up with something better? At least animals don't kill their own families. What does that make you?" Dihya curled her lip.

"Alive, bitch!"

Dihya scoffed at the man in the neighbouring cell and crouched down before Darius, a warm, sympathetic look in her eyes. A face of severe angles and full lips, she had obsidian, spiralling horns atop her thickly braided brown hair and hooked wings folded neatly behind her. The beast mage towered over him, and though her proportions were slim, she was stronger than any man he knew.

"Just lie down, Darius. I'll bring you something for the pain at the end of my shift. Won't be long now."

She was one of the few friends he'd ever truly made. One who had no interest in using him for whatever proximity to his father he could ostensibly provide. She was also the only one who could help him now.

"Nadia," he wheezed.

"I really don't think you're in any shape to see her tonight, even if I did sneak you out." Dihya frowned, keeping her words quiet.

She'd released him from prison more times than he could count since he'd met her six months ago, when Barziya had made his odious presence known in Heraklia. And she'd always snuck him back in come morning, after he'd spent the night trying unsuccessfully to woo Nadia. But he was not begging for the chance to court Nadia now—he was begging for the chance to save her life.

He had to make her understand, but he couldn't catch his breath.

"She's...in danger," he hissed through gritted teeth.

Leaning against the rough rock wall of his cell, Darius hauled himself up to a crouch. Progress.

"What in the hells are you talking about?"

"Father is...going to maim her." Darius stood on shaky legs, fighting back a wave of dizziness. Everything hurt.

Her pale complexion turned ashen.

"Shit."

"Get me out. Please, Dihya."

She shook her head, frowning.

"So you can do what? Pass out in front of her? You're in no shape to do anything."

"It's my fault. I have to warn her." He lunged forward to the bars of his cell, leaning against them. It didn't matter what shape he was in. He would crawl over a field of broken glass if it meant sparing her from what his father intended. "Please. He's sent Datis already."

"Ah, fuck me. I'm going to regret this," Dihya muttered as she turned the lock in his cell door. She caught him up in her arms, wrapping a hooked wing around him for support. "I hope you have a plan," she grumbled, taking him further into the dungeon.

In a neglected cell in the deepest section, an escape route was hidden behind mouldering crates and broken amphorae. Darius had been sent to—and escaped from—the dungeons often enough to know the way without a single light to guide him. Tonight, he needed Dihya's support to make it through the cramped, underground passage. He only hoped it wouldn't cost her too much in the end.

"I do," he lied. Once he was at Nadia's side, he would figure out a plan. Right now, he had to focus on getting to her first. Nothing else mattered.

"No, you don't. This is the plan. I get you to Nadia, and you get to the West gate while I get my family out of Heraklia. I'll get you some horses and then we part ways before your father finds out what I've done."

It was better than his nonexistent plan. He only prayed he would have the strength to carry it out.

"What now?" Nadia asked.

It was an excellent question. In his current state he'd never make it to the West gate, let alone the next block.

"Run?" he groaned, leaning most of his weight against the outer wall.

"You...you don't have a plan." She gasped, horrified. "How could you not have a plan?!"

"The plan was to get to you and get to the West gate!" he hissed, lurching off the wall, taking her hand and limping away. Dihya might be circling nearby. If he could just get Nadia to her...

"And then what?"

"Keep running? I'm figuring that part out," he said, checking round the corner to ensure the way was still clear.

"You burned my brother...on a whim? Without a real plan for what happens afterwards?" Nadia's voice was eerily calm. It raised the hairs on the nape of his neck.

"Nadia, wait..."

The scuff of a boot against the paved alleyway alerted him. They were no longer alone. One of Father's soldiers had snuck up behind them.

"What are you—"

Darius shoved her out of the way of the soldier's blade and launched a bolt of flame. But this one was not so easily deterred. Darius' flames were becoming as weak as he was. It was a stupid move. Darius braced for a close-quarters fight that never came.

Roots burst through the paved stone, piercing the soldier's legs. Up and up they grew, ripping through bones, sinew and flesh, the man's high-pitched screams of agony loud enough to wake the dead and horrifying enough to bring tears to the eyes of the cruelest foe. By the time the branches had torn through his heart, the man was silent, a gruesome broken puppet held together by twisted bark.

"Gods below..." Darius whispered, slack-jawed as he stared in horror at the bleeding corpse. "Nadia, did you...? How?"

Panting, trembling, she stared wide-eyed at the soldier, stumbling to her feet.

"I have to touch the ground to control the plants, or use my blood to... He...he was going to kill you."

Darius limped to her side.

"Come here."

He cradled her face against his chest, away from the shocking sight. She trembled in his arms. Gods, what a mess. She should never have had to do that, his feisty, precious Nadia. This was his failing, not to have come prepared with a blade of his own. Fool. The least he could do was clean up the mess.

No one could know what she'd done. Nadia was already hunted, it would be best that no one be given any other reason than the king's command to do so. He dug deep, pulling on his magical reserves to burn hot, unleashing a wave of fire at the corpse, chasing the roots through the body, rendering everything to ash and molten metal. The stench would be undeniable proof of death, but at least no one would think it by Nadia's hands.

Fearing discovery, he pulled her from the scene and limped as quickly as he could down several streets. As he watched for more soldiers, she pushed away from him, tears in her eyes.

"You're a fool to want to help me! A fool to think you alone could save me from your father's wrath! And I'm a fool to let you. Go, Darius."

His heart seized in his chest.

"No."

Her lower lip trembled.

"You saw what I did! I won't give you a choice!" she threatened.

He grabbed her by the front of her dress, dragging her closer, her eyes wide.

"If you think killing a man is going to shake my resolve, taint what I feel for you, then you don't know me."

She could burn the world to the ground and he would still yearn for her. Nadia had saved his life, and he would repay that debt for the rest of his days.

"And if you think you know me at all, then you're the greatest fool that ever lived! Now, unhand me! I can still turn myself in! I can still save my family!" She fought his hold, pressing into every hurt he'd sustained. He bit back a curse, refusing to let her go.

Nadia was wrong. He knew her—knew her heart. He could see through the fear in her eyes, the guilt, the shame. But if she'd wanted him dead, if she'd wanted to sacrifice herself, she'd have let that soldier run him through. Nadia wanted to live. And he would honour that defiant wish, her heart's true desire, above all others, no matter what else she said.

"No. And if I have to put you over my shoulder and carry you out of here, I will."

She pounded on his chest. He flinched. Fuck but he was hurting. Bravado aside, he desperately hoped she wouldn't make him carry her like a sack of angry cats. He probably wouldn't make it far.

It was only as she struggled in his arms that she noticed the blood coating her palms—his blood. His pathetic bandages were soaked through. Dihya would have one more reason to be cross with him, given she'd done her level best to keep him from bleeding everywhere.

"Darius!" She gasped.

"*Now* will you cooperate, or do you want us both to die?"

Her face twisted in sympathy and frustration. She squeezed her eyes shut and took a breath.

"Gods... Fine! Come. I know someone who owes me a favour."

"Lead the way." He released her from his hold and snagged her hand, in case she got any other foolish ideas of self-sacrifice.

He only hoped the favour owed was worth risking their lives.

CHAPTER 4

By the time they managed to get to their destination, only a few blocks from the Bladesworne home, Nadia's legs were trembling and her back slick with sweat. Already the houses were narrowing in size, the decorations plainer, the paint not nearly as new or vibrant. Nadia leaned heavily on the wall of the nearest house in the alley at its side, the better to avoid any eyes on the main street. Sweat dripping down her face and back, she grunted as she repositioned Darius. Her pulse leapt when he didn't even groan at the shifting. He'd begun to lean quite heavily on her, a thick-set warrior made of muscle, making him nearly impossible to bear. If he collapsed completely, she wasn't sure she'd be able to carry him on her own. Darius tried to mumble something, but his words were slurred, his head hanging heavily.

The sun was nearly set, allowing them to more easily hide in the shadows. After checking the main street up and down, Nadia knocked on the door of the small townhouse. Once the blue paint had been as deep as the ocean, but the owner had long since stopped with the expense, leaving a faded pale blue which barely covered up the painted sign underneath for a healer no longer in residence. After an anxious wait, constantly looking over her shoulder for pursuers and watchful eyes, the great door creaked open, revealing a servant in a cream tunic. Behind her, in the entryway, a short, stocky redheaded woman with wide dark eyes and freckled skin greeted her with a horrified expression.

"Nobilissima Verdant, what are you doing here?"

"I'm calling in my favour, Akeso. Please, allow us inside."

The woman looked at the state of her attire and the blood crusted on her hands and trickling down Darius' side, his head hanging down, black hair escaping its confines. Then her eyes went to the streets. Seeing no onlookers, she allowed them entry. The first room was blessedly just around the corner from the entryway, a small, windowless place with a simple bed and a few furnishings.

When at last Nadia was able to lay Darius down, she leaned against the nearest wall, head and heart pounding, muscles screaming their protest at the abuse.

"Watch where you touch, Nobilissima, you'll get blood on the frescos." Akeso called from another room as she ordered servants to fetch her towels, boiled water and clean clothes.

The walls of the room were painted simply in panels of bright colours with the odd decorative florals or animals in the centre. Nadia sat on the edge of the small bed she'd managed to heave Darius onto, her head in her hands. What in the hells was she supposed to do now? Where could she even go?

Akeso interrupted her morose musings and shooed her aside. She passed a damp cloth to Nadia, nodding at her hands. Nadia cleaned herself off, then made to wipe the blood off of the parts of Darius she could easily reach.

"Go, rest, I can take care of the soldier. One of my servants will have a bath and new clothes ready for you," Akeso said.

Nadia heeded her, leaving Darius to the healer. Female healers rarely became more than midwives in Lethe, but being noble-born, even that had been denied Akeso. A blessing in disguise for Nadia, as it'd meant Firetongue hadn't found out about her gift—or that she'd been studying the art of healing since her marriage.

The bath water was cold, but much appreciated. She didn't bother to linger, happy to trade her ash-smudged, blood-spattered frock for a simple, clean gown.

It was as she was plaiting her braids that Akeso stormed into the room and shooed the servants away, her thunderous expression reflected in the polished bronze mirror.

"What is the meaning of this?"

Shit.

"How dare you bring one of *his* people into my home! After what he did to my boys?! And not just one of his soldiers, the same son who dragged them to the warfront! Explain yourself, Nadia!" Akeso's face was red, fists shaking at her side in her rage.

Nadia turned around to face the healer, voice as calm and level as she could make it while her heart galloped in her chest.

"King Firetongue has called for my maiming. Prince Darius risked his life to save me."

"And you thought it a good idea to bring him and your trouble to my door?! Get out!"

Akeso had every reason to throw her out, but Nadia could not allow it to happen. It didn't matter how shamelessly she needed to act at that moment. Her life and Darius' were on the line. Nadia narrowed her eyes and squared her shoulders.

"Not before Darius is healed."

"You're in no position to make demands of me. You should be grateful I haven't thrown you out and alerted the city guard!" Akeso stamped her foot.

"I have every right to make demands, Akeso." Nadia stood, hazel eyes glaring the woman into retreat. The closer Nadia stepped to the woman, the less haughty the healer's posture, the less fiery her outrage. Yes, Darius' presence was an insult, but Akeso owed her. "Without me, your family, your dependents, your servants, your horses and cattle, they all would have starved. You'd have been forced to give up your jewels, your home—everything. And that is not the only thing I've done for you. I've kept your secret safe. If the King knew you were a healer, you'd have been sent to the frontlines with your boys, the target of every heartless enemy assassin looking for an easy way to cripple Arcadia's fighting forces. But I kept your secret and I ensured you had a steady supply of tight-lipped, wealthy clientele to keep your estates flush while your sons and husband served the King. You. Owe. Me."

Akeso glared, cowed, but not for long.

"Fine. But after this, my debts are paid. You should have submitted yourself to him. I could have healed you if he'd blinded you, slit your nose or burned you. I've done the same for others he's punished. But you've likely enraged him now. And no healer can regrow a severed nose, a limb, a tongue...or a head."

"So be it," Nadia replied, refusing to allow Akeso to see even a single revealing tremor. "I'll remain with Darius until he wakes."

The better to ensure the healer did as she promised.

Nadia followed Akeso back to Darius' side and watched her work, an eye on her at all times. When she was done, his bruises, cuts and gashes were healed, only the dried blood of his wounds remained, staining his torn, singed tunic and drying on his skin. Akeso left without another word, leaving towels, water and a fresh set of clothes behind. Nadia took it upon herself to finish the task of cleaning him up, dipping the cloth into the bowl of water. As she ran it across his hairline, she held back tears. He looked so boyish as he slept, peaceful. And yet he was a whirlwind wreaking havoc on her life, her plans, her resolve. She would never have been put in this position had he not showed up in her life.

But she would never have known this strange, wonderful, terrible feeling that had permeated her very bones. A feeling that drove her to distraction whenever he was near. A feeling that made her yearn for him whenever he was away. A feeling she'd killed to protect.

It wasn't love, but it felt perilously close. And it couldn't have come at a worse time. *Love leads to ruin.* Her mother's remonstrations rang in her ears, her father's stern look as he told her exactly what he expected of her haunted her. As the eldest daughter, she was to be a role model for her younger sisters. Every slip of her tongue had meant a slap in the face. Every imperfect dance step had been met with the punishment of fifty flawless repetitions. And all of it had been couched as for her benefit. Her future husband would expect no less, and his punishments would be much more severe. Until now, whenever she was watched, Nadia had been the perfect daughter, or as close to perfect as any mage could be. *Love leads to ruin.* Now, there was no going back. She'd suffered all that time, screaming on the inside, and she'd thrown it all away for the rogue in front of her.

As she struggled to remove his ruined tunic, she pushed her fears down, somewhere deep and dark where they couldn't turn her into a scared, helpless, wailing child. Now was the time to plan. Where in Lethe could they go? The whole of the continent was at war, but some places were safer than others. The highlands of the Aeolian islands were rumoured to be mostly untouched, but its coastline was another story.

Finally with his tunic off, she could clean the sticky blood from his torso. Swallowing hard to calm her racing pulse, she set to work, doing her best to keep her mind on the matter at hand, rather than the feel of his skin and the distracting sight of his chest hair. She'd never seen a man wearing so little. Nobles both low and high took pride in how well-sheltered they kept their women, and it was only by Darius' bold stubbornness that she'd secretly met with him and tended his minor scrapes before. But he'd always had his clothes on...

Focus.

They could also try their luck in the kingdom of Temenos. No army had successfully breached the swamps on its land borders, and King Calypsos might be convinced to help them install Darius in King Barziya's place, provided Darius made a Queen of one of Calypsos' many daughters. Better Nadia be forced into the role of concubine than die, and at the very least she would still be near enough to real power to make a difference in Lethe.

"You know, I'm almost hurt."

Nadia gasped. He held her hands in place on his chest, refusing to let her pull away. Thank the gods, he was awake.

"How do you feel?" she asked, searching his face.

"Irate. Is my body so unappealing that your mind is wandering?"

"I meant physically." She pursed her lips, frowning.

"Hmmm..." he mused, "I'd feel better if your hands were lower."

"My...hands?"

He smiled, a wolfish grin making her cheeks heat as he slid her hands closer to his loincloth, running her fingers over a thick trail of coarse hair that disappeared beneath. Thankfully he stopped at his belly button, but it was far too close for comfort.

"Your beautiful, delicate hands. Every part of you is soft, silky perfection, Nadia."

She gasped.

"Oh! You loathsome brute! Let go of my wrists," she hissed.

He released her immediately, but before she could stand, or maybe hit him with the cloth, he pulled her close, wrapping his strong arms around her.

"Darius—"

"Shhh, just let me hold you a moment. Just...let my mind catch up to my eyes. I need to know you're not some ghost sent to torment me for failing you."

Gone was the flirt. At his slight tremble and shaky breath, she relaxed in his arms, throwing her own around him and holding him close, as if his mere presence could banish her fears.

"You didn't fail me," she murmured.

He pushed her up, just enough so he could search her face with a bewildered expression.

"No, now I know this is a dream. The Nadia I know would have torn me to shreds with her words alone." He chuckled. "And if that's the case, would you like to remove your—"

She flicked his ear hard enough to make him flinch.

"Ah, not a dream then."

Nadia pushed off him entirely and handed him the spare tunic. Gods, was he so incapable of letting a single moment pass without a prank?

"Put this on."

He sighed dramatically but did as he was told. Once he was decent, she collected her wits, forced down her terror and faced him.

"We need a plan and we don't have a lot of time to concoct one. We are supposed to leave the premises the moment you wake up."

The sun had set since they'd arrived. Hopefully the darkness would be their ally.

Darius flexed his hand and patted his side.

"I would say your friend's favour didn't extend very far, but given how good I feel, I'm not really in a place to cast aspersions."

"Do you have anywhere safe we can go, Darius?"

He rubbed a hand over his face, shaking his head.

"None that my father doesn't know about, I'm afraid. But if it's safety you need, there's always the Temple of the Undying Flame."

Her face mirrored her disgust.

"But only eccentric cultists and political outcasts go there!"

Not to mention, anyone who sought refuge there was expected to serve, and serving meant giving up ties to worldly politics...and power. It was why no king had ever interfered with the Temple and allowed its priests and priestesses limited independence. She could not accept that. Not after everything she'd worked for.

"Nadia, we *are* political outcasts. We were, the moment my father called for your maiming and I acted against him. At least at the Temple, we'll be safe."

Safe and forever rendered powerless and irrelevant. The very fate she'd been fighting against her whole life.

"We could flee to the islands, to another kingdom!"

Hells, she'd rather leave Lethe altogether if the Temple were to be her fate here. At least abroad she could recoup, plan and most importantly, return.

"Nadia," Darius put a hand on her shoulder, his eyes solemn and sad. "We'll be lucky if we make it out of the city alive, luckier still to make it all the way to the Temple unharmed. I fled with nothing but the clothes on my back. We've no coin for sea travel or a long, overland journey, unless you're willing to rob fellow travellers. I'll do it, if that's what you truly desire, but I don't think you do."

He was right, of course. She would not stoop to the level of a bandit, terrorizing people already shouldering the burdens and horrors of war. But she'd already killed a man, a line she never thought she'd personally cross. If she could so easily disregard the life of another when it suited her, how long would her good intentions hold out when faced with the possibility of living her own personal nightmare?

Nadia sighed, defeated. For now. If she lived long enough to confront a life of forced insignificance, she could worry about it then. At present, they had more pressing concerns.

"Alright, then how do you propose we escape?"

CHAPTER 5

Darius had long dreamed of what he would do if he ever had the chance to whisk Nadia away from the protective grasp of her family. He would take her to the races, maybe a play, have the cook make her favourite foods and then take her on a picnic somewhere charming and bucolic, perhaps take her boating on a lake, hells even a tour of the marketplace where he could buy her a pretty new necklace she could wear.

But no. The fates were cruel and the world unjust. Though they walked hand in hand, there was no romance in the act. The alleys were cramped, barely wide enough for one man to proceed through. Gods help them if they had to pass another poor soul, or they'd be forced to squeeze so close to each other their noses would be sure to touch. No, instead of playing a gallant prince and pampered noblissima, they were dodging rotting refuse and the contents of neglected, oozing public latrines as they neared Heraklia's West gate. Unscrupulous landlords had long ago built a maze of cramped apartment blocks, now crumbling and filled to bursting with the city's less illustrious denizens. It didn't help that they'd needed to keep clear of all major thoroughfares to avoid being spotted by groups of royal guards scouring the streets.

Darius did his best to remain on the outskirts of the narrow web of alleys, yet just far enough from the city walls to avoid the few patrols that walked them at this hour. Datis hadn't yet doubled up on the wall patrol. A blessing. Perhaps Father didn't yet know they had escaped, else the whole city would have been locked down.

Only another half block and they'd be at the gates. Sweat dripped down his back despite the chill night air.

Please gods let the gate guards be lax.

"Darius!" Nadia hissed a warning.

A guard had just turned down the cramped alley behind them. If he raised the alarm, they'd never make it out of the alley, never mind the city gates. Darius pushed past Nadia and rushed the guard. The man wasn't half as well-trained as the royal guards. Instead of reaching for his magic, he reached for his sword. Instead of crying out, he fought in the cramped quarters, intent on being the first to attack. But just as he couldn't afford for the man to raise the alarm, Darius couldn't use his magic either by launching streamers of fire here, where every dry, crumbling bit of wood would instantly light. The overcrowded apartment blocks would quickly become a grizzly funeral pyre, trapping all who dwelt within.

Just before the guard thought to cry out to his fellows patrolling the nearest street, Darius grabbed his mouth and blasted fire down his throat and up his nose, hot enough to melt the guard's innards before he could scream. The man collapsed, stinking of cooked flesh and singed hair. Had anyone heard? Seen? He turned to Nadia. Eyes wide and hand over her mouth, she stared at him in horror and awe.

"Are you alright?"

She nodded, speechless for the first time since he'd known her. What a waste to have it be because of a little murder. He sighed.

"Keep a look out. I'm going to strip him of his armour. Let's pray it fits."

Stripping the guard was harder than he'd imagined and every clink and clang of the metal set his heart to racing, but, blessedly, no one discovered them. Deed done, he hauled the body to the nearest pile of filth and tossed it over, using a half-broken pot shard to shovel some refuse atop. Even here, a fresh corpse would incite curiosity. He donned the armour in record time, wincing at the belts biting into him. Darius appeared as nothing so much as a sausage nearly bursting its casing, but he hoped no one would notice in the dark. At least he now had a sword and a dagger.

With a helmet, he would blend with the guards. But what of Nadia?

He grinned.

"How would you like to play a part?"

No nobilissima would walk the streets near the West gate of Heraklia. No merchant or noble servant would either, and certainly not at night.

"What do you mean?"

"I doubt many of the guards would recognize you on sight. They're looking for a noblewoman. And with a few touches..." He reached out to her robe. "May I?"

"If you must."

He removed her robe and pulled down the neckline of her gown, then, finding it to be not quite the desired effect, took his blade and split the neckline of her gown. Before she could protest he raised a finger to silence her.

"A torn gown is mended with a lot more ease than a severed artery. They're looking for a prince and a noblewoman, not a guard and a prostitute. If I ask to be let outside the gates for privacy, they might just grant it."

"Gods below. This had better work, or I will-"

"Save it until we're free of the gates."

Her mutinous glare brought a smile to his face. Better she find her anger than dwell on the horrors of the night. There would be time for that soon enough. Provided they survived. Together, they stepped closer to the main thoroughfare, away from the body of the guard and the worst of the smells.

"Now, sway your hips a bit more as you walk and cling to my arm. And for the love of the gods, don't cover up your cleavage."

Oh, he was going to pay for that, if the fire in her eyes was any indication. But that was a problem for the Darius who survived this wild gambit, not for the one trying to pull it off.

CHAPTER 6

Was Darius...*enjoying this?*

He unbraided her hair, letting it flow down her back, running his fingers through the long tresses. Despite the dire urgency of their situation, he seemed determined not to rush this aspect. Was it really so necessary? Their ruse merely needed to be adequate.

"We don't have time for this," she protested.

"Look at me, Nadia."

He chuckled at her glare.

"Look at me like you want me."

"I...I'm not sure how."

Maybe they did need to prepare. Darius always provoked her ire, and purposefully. Then he would lean in for stolen touches and heated glances. She'd never...allowed herself the luxury of staring at him longingly. It would only have earned her another lecture, another slap, another lesson on how she could be no less than the perfect specimen of noble womanhood.

"Be still my heart, you really do know how to stroke a man's ego." He rolled his eyes.

Anger heated her cheeks as much as embarrassment.

"This won't work! Maybe I should act like I'm ill?"

"Then why in Lethe would a guard be helping you outside the gates? No." He looked at her mouth, then grinned, his eyes full of promise. "You've been taught all your life how to live like a noblewoman, always expected to stifle your passions, your thoughts, every fiery, beautiful part of you. Do you want to know what it's like to feel passion? Freely? Unreservedly?"

Her heart leapt. Despite his constant needling, his arrogance, his propensity for taking up too much of everything—space, air, her thoughts—Darius always seemed to see the heart of her. She hated him for it. Nadia was more accustomed to hiding herself, to only showing what she meant to show. To know that another could see through her so easily was deeply unsettling. But did she want passion—a wild, reckless thing to quiet her racing mind, to set fire to all her rules, to her façade? She swallowed.

"In future, perhaps, and not when our lives are on the line."

"If not now, you may never get another chance."

Nadia turned her face away, so that he couldn't see her resolve waver.

"And how exactly is this going to help?"

"If you don't know passion, how can you mimic it?"

He crowded her against the brick of the city's outer wall. He traced a finger across the back of her hand, up her arm and across her collarbone, his touch sending a frisson through her. Another hot hand pulled her close at the waist before snaking down to her rear. His ruby eyes devoured her. Gods below.

"If you don't like something, you tell me to stop," he whispered in her ear before he took the lobe between his teeth and tugged.

Her breath left her in a sharp gasp. She bit her lips, lest he stop in truth.

Darius kissed his way up and down her neck, one hand anchoring her head, the other pulling her closer than anyone had ever held her. Her mind rebelled, unsure why any of this felt good, but her traitorous body leaned into every touch, greedy for this heady sensation. Without knowing, her hands gripped his hard body.

And then his lips found hers. Her first kiss. It was intoxicating, the softness of his lips and the scrape of his beard. His tongue along the seam of her lips had her gasping. Showing her no mercy, his tongue touched hers, sliding along it, sending a shiver down her spine. Nadia pulled him close, desperate for more, to chase this feeling down whatever path it took her. Before she could discover more, feel more, he pulled away. Breathless, their eyes locked. Nadia didn't know who she was anymore, only that she wanted every part of her pressed to every part of him.

He kissed her again, harder, rougher, his fist gripping the material of her dress, as lost as she. Or at least, that's what she'd thought. He pulled away again, groaning.

"When we're free of the place, so help me, I won't let it end with a kiss, Nadia."

The timber of his voice created an ache in her core. Heart pounding in her chest, she nodded, unable to form words.

"Now that you know something of passion, maybe we can pull this off."

He pulled her along the street, heading for the gates as her head spun. Gods below, no wonder they'd kept her and all her sisters supervised while potential suitors were about. If she'd known what Darius' playful caresses could have become months ago... *Love leads to ruin.*

But now was not the time to fantasize. She did as he'd instructed, swaying her hips in an unladylike fashion, letting her gown reveal more of her breasts than she'd ever contemplated, and glued herself to his side, petting his arm and fawning over him. Darius, for his part, played the consummate lecher, his eyes never straying above her collarbones.

They passed three guards on the street, and not a single one bothered to look at her face. She supposed she must be grateful for that. It took everything in her not to pull the torn material of décolletage together and hiss at the men leering at her.

"You're swaying your hips so violently it's like they're trying to escape your body. Tone it down," he whispered through a false smile.

What a perfectly dreadful thing to say.

"How would I know how to walk like a prostitute when I've never seen one before?" she asked him in a hushed, sing-song voice.

"Fine, scrap the walk, just smile and push your tits up on my arm."

How skillfully he made an irritant of himself. She couldn't believe she'd let him talk her into kissing him.

"I'm going to geld you when this is over." She smiled, batting her lashes as she complied, gritting her teeth.

"You'd have to touch my cock to geld me, love. And the moment you see it, you'll be moved to spare me. I'm told it's one of my best features." He winked.

It took an effort of great will not to recoil from his crude language.

"If it's on par with your wit, then it seems the bar has been set in the deepest of hells"

And of course he grinned at her. Did he relish being insulted, challenged? Why was this man so fascinated with every unladylike barb that came from her mouth?

Whatever the case was, it would have to wait. They approached the gates, where two guards stood at attention next to torches, the way shut. The doors soared overhead, taller than three men standing atop each other's shoulders and wide enough for four chariots to roll through with ease. Made of thick wood, the doors, like the outer casing of the walls, were enchanted to dispel magic. It was a testament to Heraklia's obscene former wealth that such enchantments protected the city.

"Let me do the talking."

Nadia kept a lazy smile plastered on her face as Darius began his conversation with the guard, until the guard screamed Darius' name. Between one word and the next, Darius grabbed the guard and swung him to the side. Hot blood splashed Nadia's face as two arrows pierced the soldier through. Using the guard as a shield, Darius pushed her behind him and backed up towards the gate.

"Can you open the gate? I'll cover you!"

The gates of the city were closed at night and only opened by internal mechanisms operated by levers from the inside, but it usually took the strength of a soldier to crank them. As the hue and cry went up, Nadia's panic would have to substitute for strength. She pulled with all her might, barely able to make it budge. As she strained to move it, Darius pulled her from her task and dove out of the way. A ball of flame came down from the walls above. Heat seared her side, and her gown was set alight. As quickly as the fire had caught, Darius used his mage gift to douse it. It seemed it would be her only reprieve.

The lever was red hot and dripping molten metal, the mechanism melted into place. There would be no escape.

The echoing of hooves on cobblestone was their death knell.

Gods below, they were going to die horrible deaths.

King Barziya would torture her for days, weeks, maybe even longer, just to slake his anger. She would be begging for death long before the end.

"Nadia!" Darius shook her, bringing her back. "Don't you dare let them take you alive. Anything you have to do to survive, you do it. Promise me!"

"Darius, I—"

He grabbed the dead soldier's shield, saving them from another volley of arrows. The archer's were on the walls, pinning them down as reinforcements arrived.

"No! What you did to that soldier? You do that until you've drained your magic dry. If you want to live, you have to become a monster. It's you or them, Nadia. Who are you going to fight for?"

But the harder she fought, the worse it would be for her, for her family. What if the king's ire spread to them as well?

"What about my family? If I fight back..."

"The family who loves you already sacrificed their skin so you could escape. Honour that sacrifice and live!"

Her brother's screams rang in her ears. As more arrows rained down upon them, Darius held her close.

"I can't do this without you, Nadia. If you give up, if you die, I die."

She swallowed. Her heart rebelled against the very notion. She didn't want that. Never that.

"What am I supposed to do?"

He grinned, a feral, vicious thing.

"My brother will be the one on the horse. The second he dismounts, you run him through with your plants and you do it as fast as possible. He's the strongest mage here and his attention will be on me. If he dies, the rest will think twice. After that, protect yourself. I can take care of the others."

Ah gods, it was the worst plan she'd ever taken part in. But it was their only chance save defeat and death. It would have to do. But if she were to grow something so quickly, she would need to bleed. If she were to create another vicious tree, breathe terrible life into it, she had to have life to give it. This was no fertile field with seeds sown in rich soil, waiting for her magic to help it along, her hands or feet touching the earth and allowing her to use her magic with ease. The gardens of the well-to-do were far off. There wasn't even a sickly tree nearby to offer shade. The cobbles blocked out all but the hardiest weeds and the soil here was poor, hard-packed and devoid of the kind of plants she needed. Here, if she wanted to create life, she had to give it life.

The clack of horseshoes on cobble finally came to a stop, as did the constant pelting of arrows, lodging themselves in Darius' shield. Nadia reached up to that same shield and cut deep in the side of her arm, letting her blood soak between the cobbles. She looked to Darius, determined. He pulled her close for one last kiss.

Hard and fast and desperate, it ended so quickly she might have thought it a dream.

"Darius, just come along quietly and hand over the whore. You know you're not getting out of here and neither is she. We've had the gates watched and the walls manned for the past hour waiting for you. It'll be better for everyone if you just give up," Datis said from atop his horse.

"Ready?" Darius whispered to her.

Her blood had soaked into the earth, a seed germinating from the life she fed it, magic spurring it on, stretching tendrils beneath the soil.

"Yes."

Darius stood carefully, his eyes on the archers, on his brother, on the small contingent of soldiers that had arrived. How in the gods unknowable names was he supposed to take on so many alone?

"Oh, really? You mean to tell me King Barziya is capable of mercy? Did he learn it in the last hour? How fortuitous."

Datis scowled, readying to dismount. Nadia pulled on her magic, already depleted from earlier. The moment he set foot on the ground, he would be dead.

"She's no one. You're a prince. Let Father cut her up and get on with your life. There are plenty more where she came from."

"And if I don't, what will you do? Kill me? And let precious Firetongue blood seep into the cobbles in this gods-forsaken shithole? That's right!" He scanned the crowd, all bravado and bluster. "The lot of you are lucky none of you have spilled a drop of royal blood this eve! You may attack me on my father's orders now, but will he protect you tomorrow, a week from now, when I have my revenge? Will he even remember giving the order? Will he even know who you are? No one is going to protect you from me when this is done. No one." He sneered. The archers lowered their bows, the soldiers looked to each other. Gods below, was this actually working? Darius turned to Datis and raised his brow. "If you want me to come peacefully, you'll have to come and get me." Darius grinned, his arms open wide, strategically covering her with his shield.

Datis scoffed, but, seeing the hesitancy of his soldiers, swung his leg over his horse.

"Stand down. Leave him to me."

He touched the toe of his boot to the ground. Nadia struck. Piercing the leather of his boot and then his foot, her branch tore up through the ground. He doubled over and her branch ripped through Datis' heart, bursting out the back of his armour, showering the horse with blood . It reared up in a panic, crumpling the helmet of the nearest soldier before it took off through the narrow streets.

Darius didn't waste a single moment. While the soldiers were struck with horror and awe, he launched a wave of flame at the top of the wall, chasing archer after archer until not a single one had been spared his flames. As Datis' horse sped off, Darius rushed for the fallen soldier's blade and shield, taking on the nearest stupefied guard with unmatched fury. Some of the soldiers fled, the rest hesitated before joining the mad melee. Magic flew in earnest then, shards of ice, blades of wind and the crackle of lightning, all joined the molten sweep of fire. These were the gifts most mages in Lethe had, the ones so coveted by the elementalists and nobility alike.

Nadia was fading fast, but she would not let him fight alone. While Darius pushed them further from her position by the gate, she watched the melee. The lightning mage was the most dangerous. Clad in thick leathers and carrying a whip, if he stopped caring about the lives of his fellow soldiers, he could electrocute every man in metal armour, Darius included. She sent tendrils of her magic out, squeezing blood from her arm, feeding her plant the life it needed to grow. Striking out, she missed as the mage lashed out in the melee. But he'd seen her branch now, his eyes tracing the source back to her. He raised his arm, readying himself to end her life, a bright crackling magic in his hand. A sword ran through his side. As Darius withdrew, Nadia realized her error. He'd overextended himself to save her.

As if time itself had slowed, she watched in horror as two separate blades made to run him through. He might be able to parry one, but not the other. She'd doomed him to die. As he turned to do just that, an arrow cut through the skies, embedding itself in the neck of the opposite soldier. One more wave of flame and a brutal thrust later, and the last remaining soldier was dead.

But just because they'd killed their way through this batch, didn't mean more weren't coming. Bells were ringing in the distance, and not a single citizen was sleeping.

"Dihya! You saved my hide!" Darius smiled, his face awash in blood.

"I'm always saving your hide." The winged beast mage touched down beside Nadia. The woman held out her hand to help her up. "But this is the last time."

Before she could protest, Dihya had Nadia in her lithe, muscled arms and was taking flight, up and over the wall, where two horses waited, small packs attached to their saddles. A moment later, and Darius was set down beside her.

"Thank you," Nadia said, eyes wide.

Dihya waved her off, scowling.

"I didn't think they would guard the West gate. I'm sorry I took so long. It was harder than I thought to round up my siblings and get them out. Our favourite silver-tongue scum apparently squealed, so the king had already discovered you got out on my watch, hence the extra gate security. Now, if you'll excuse me, I need to flee. You can thank me by not dying."

"Best of luck, my friend." Darius waved as the beast mage took flight once more, disappearing in the night skies.

"We...we made it out," Nadia whispered, shaking as Darius helped her seat the horse.

"Of the city. We're not safe yet."

No, they wouldn't be safe until they reached the Temple of the Undying Flame. Where all her hopes, dreams and ambitions would go to die so that she could live.

CHAPTER 7

Darius could barely believe his luck in surviving Heraklia. Such luck was a gift he wouldn't soon forget, and for which he would offer thanks to the forgotten gods as soon as he had proper libations to dedicate. As he'd seated his horse and urged Nadia's into a canter, it had taken an effort of will not to shake. He'd never been one to shy from battle, but he'd never faced odds quite so unfavourable before.

Nadia's countenance was bloodless as she gripped the reins, focusing solely on the hard ride ahead. If not for her willingness to use her mage gift for violent ends and Dihya's unwavering loyalty, things might not have gone so well. Darius owed both women his life several times over.

They rode through the night, pushing their horses as hard and fast as they could, faster than was wise when only the moon and stars illuminated the dirt road. Their luck held, and neither horse hit a potentially lethal pothole in the dark. Before long though, the poor beasts were barely plodding along. Only then did they turn off the main road, following the sounds of running water, trudging deep enough into the treeline so as not to be spotted. They dared not light a fire. Darius grimaced. It was going to be a cold night.

Dihya had packed them the bare essentials for a getaway; rations for a few days and a crudely drawn map to the Temple. It was enough to get them to their destination if they stayed the course. But if Dihya thought the Temple their only escape, that meant Father would as well.

Nadia was swaying on her feet as she led the horses to the nearby stream. Darius pitched their tent and tossed the blankets inside, feeling every ache and a bone-deep weariness. When Nadia returned to tie their horses up for the few hours till sunrise, she paused.

"Is that...?"

"Our bed."

She appeared unconvinced.

"Surely, you're jesting."

He grinned. So his pampered nobilissima could deal with bloodshed, murder and treason, but not a makeshift bed?

"Do you see any plush inns in these woods, Nobilissima?"

"But...you'll be in there...with me?"

"Well, the tent is mine and if you don't think you can keep your hands off me, you can sleep outside for the sake of my virtue."

"Don't be an ass."

Darius nearly growled. They were in no position to be choosy about their accommodations and he was not a beast who would paw at her in the night unbidden. Just the thought of it made him ill. That was something his father might do, but Darius prided himself on being a man with a gods damned conscience, at least when women were involved. His strides ate up the distance between them. To her credit, she refused to retreat, despite her blush.

"We can't afford to light a fire, not this close to the city and the main road. Despite your insinuations, I would never harm you. But I'm not so much of a gentleman that I'm going to willingly freeze for a few hours. I need to sleep, as do you."

More's the pity. He finally had her all to himself, no meddlesome family for miles, and yet he barely had the energy to have this conversation, let alone seduce her with the finesse she required.

"I don't think you'd ever hurt me," she whispered.

"Gods below, something we finally agree on," he grumbled, though the admission went a very long way to soothing his hurt.

"It's just sleeping. Nothing more," she warned him, pressing her full lips in a mulish line, daring him to say differently.

He supposed he deserved that, given he was an unapologetic flirt where she was concerned.

"Nadia, if I'm going to do more with you, believe me, you'll know. *And* you'll be begging me for it." He forced a grin. There would be no question about her enthusiastic willingness when time came for it.

"I won't beg for anything." She scowled, breezing past him and all but throwing herself into the tent.

He repressed a chuckle, following her inside. Now, she'd all but ensured that he would most certainly make her beg for it. Settling next to her, he pulled her close. She pushed at him, gasping indignantly.

"What do you think—"

"How did you think we were going to stay warm?"

She frowned, no longer pushing him away, but not letting him any closer.

"The tent is keeping out the wind and the blankets—"

"The tent's best days were a decade ago and the blankets will barely cover us. Keeping close is our best hope for warmth."

"Now I know you're just being a pest for the sake of it." She glared.

Pulling the cover over herself, she left him without a stitch of fabric. He pulled it back, leaving her backside in the cold in retaliation.

"Of the two of us, who here has spent a single night outside a comfortable bedchamber?"

Nadia wracked her mind for a suitable retort as she gripped her corner of the blanket, pulling it taught. It did nothing but allow a cold current to come between them.

"Surely your accommodations were always the finest. You're a prince."

He could see the cold affecting her now, the gooseflesh trailing up her arms. Maybe the triumph he felt made him less of a gentleman than he'd first thought.

"One prince among more than a dozen, and the least loved of the lot," he replied, tweaking her nose. Not that there had been any love to be had in his father's palace, not once Mother died. "Besides, I had to train as a strategos, the same as any other. The only one with fancy accommodations on a march was my father and whichever brother of mine licked his boots the hardest that day. Everyone else camped like regular soldiers."

He pulled her close again, draping the blanket over them. Nearly nose to nose, the fabric only just covered them both.

"Did you huddle for warmth then as well?" she asked, her voice like acid. Still, she didn't push him away.

Only on the nights he invited women to his tent, and then the huddling was more for fun than necessity. But Nadia didn't need to know that.

"Rarely, because we could light fires or pay for warmth charms. Now go to sleep, Nadia. The moment you wake, we'll be back on the horses."

Gods, if only he'd had any aptitude at enchantment. But he was a conjurer, through and through. He could summon a flame from nothing, shape it to his will with consummate skill, but ask him to enchant something not to burn or to create even the smallest amount of heat without a flame and he was useless.

"Just admit you're full of it, Darius."

Did she know she'd just gripped the fabric of his tunic, as if clutching him? Probably not. Best not to mention it. Maybe she didn't think so poorly of him after all.

"Just admit you're protesting for the sake of it, Nadia."

She shivered. He almost smiled, and not because she was cold, but because she moved closer to him of her own volition, curling into him.

In any other circumstance, he'd have layered on the charm. But as tired, sore and worried as he was, it was simply...nice. Darius had blessed few things in his life that were simply nice.

"I'm only cold because you cut my gown."

"Of course."

As she drifted off in his arms, the smile slipped from his lips. He'd almost lost her today more times than he cared to count. The moment his father had threatened her, some feral part of him had taken over, guided his hand to his father's dagger, telling him where to plant it. Barziya had taken enough from him for one lifetime; his childhood, his mother, his peace—he would not take Nadia, too. He'd known it for so long but refused to say it aloud, but in every fibre of his being the truth was plain—Darius loved her.

From the moment he'd met her, he'd lost himself in her hazel eyes. From the very first pointed barb she'd shot his way, he'd known something deep inside him would never be the same. Her very presence had reshaped him, had given him hope his heart would find the thing he'd never had—a home.

In the few unguarded moments she'd gifted him, his heart was whole. He could not care less for his title, and even less for his remaining family. The Temple would be good for them—a respite from the outside, from all the politicking and the bloodshed. He would finally be rid of his father, no longer afraid that one day, he'd be broken by Barziya's violence and become like him, despite his best efforts. That alone made everything he'd suffered worthwhile.

They might never accomplish more than sweeping the Temple's forgotten corners or tending its gardens, but if they made it there alive, they would have each other for the rest of their lives. For him, there was no greater gift. Freed from the pressures and expectations of their families, they could simply be Darius and Nadia, a good for nothing who loved a beautiful, fiercely intelligent woman with all his heart.

So long as they were alive and together, the world would be good and right.

As he, too, drifted off, he memorized the feel of her in his arms. If today was his last day, he wanted to die remembering what it felt like to hold Nadia, the warmth of her skin, the even cadence of her breaths, the soft slide of her hair, the trust she begrudgingly bestowed. Maybe, if he were lucky, he'd live long enough to see the love he felt reflected in her eyes.

CHAPTER 8

The next several days passed in a blur of aching muscles and gut-wrenching anxiety. Nadia had never travelled so hard and so long on horseback before. She'd barely had the energy to protest when Darius held her close at night, and as the days and nights wore on, she found herself less and less inclined to do so. He'd never once taken liberties and, despite her misgivings over his aims, he'd spoken truth. Without his warmth, she might have frozen during the nights.

They'd chanced going into the closest market town for supplies, trading her jewelry and his ill-fitted armour for whatever coin they could to provision themselves. Their pursuers had ensured the main roads were watched, forcing them to take lesser travelled, longer paths to their destination. It meant they had to travel twice as fast to make it the same distance. When at last the Temple towered on the horizon, the noontime sun baking the earth in a shimmery haze, sick dread gnawed at her.

Unlike every other building in Lethe, the Temple of the Undying Flame eschewed colour and beauty. While the parts open to the public were made of sterile, white stone, undecorated columns reaching high while its floors were simple dark tiles, the main temple itself was entirely unique. Rising out of the flat, fertile plain and visible for great distances, the Temple stood, a stone monolith of truly breathtaking size. It was easily as large as a palace, and it was said that the flame resided in the centre, the inner temple carved into the rock itself. No one knew for certain, of course, as those who were allowed to enter never left the Temple nor revealed its secrets.

Nadia's hands tightened on her reins. It was effectively a prison, and any sane person understood that. As they turned off the road and into the forest, her heart hammered in her chest.

"We'll stop here for the day and make the rest of the journey after dark, when the main road isn't being patrolled. It'll take us most of the night, but if we time it right, we'll arrive before the sun rises and the first patrols begin," Darius announced, hopping off his horse and offering his hand to help her do the same.

She knew his hand like she knew her own now. Rough from calluses, warm and strong, capable of terrible violence and shocking gentleness. Though she yearned to take them, to gaze into eyes that loved her every day, she couldn't. If she took his hand now, if she let him lead her to the Temple, the life she'd schemed for, the ambitions she'd harboured, the world she wanted to create—it would all be for naught. The woman Nadia wanted to be might as well be dead. She would never be happy sweeping courtyards and tending the sacred orchards.

As much as she'd come to care for Darius, as much as she wanted more with him, if she resented her life, the situation his attentions had mired her in, what hope was there for real feelings to blossom? Bitterness would creep into her roots and rot her from the inside out. She would rather face a hundred tyrants, live knowing the axe could fall at any moment, than spend a long life slowly dying of a poisoned heart.

"Nadia?" Darius looked up at her, stretching out his hand.

He must have seen the decision in her eyes then, her hesitation giving way to determination. His grip circled her ankle as his eyes narrowed in warning.

"Nadia, don't you d—"

She panicked, spurring her horse onward, lashing out at his hand with her whip as her horse took off running. Branches clawed at her face as she leaned down, pressing her cheek to the horse's neck. Once free of the forest, open fields allowed her to push her mount as fast as it could go. Nadia knew this area, knew the roads. She didn't have to sentence herself to a life at the Temple.

Barziya knew their intended destination, but if she turned towards the Flatlands Pass, her family's stronghold, would he dare put his soldiers there? Would he risk having to potentially war with King Dragonsblood just to maim her? Because Strategos Illyia, one of Dragonsblood's, would soon arrive in her territory, eager to pillage while his master's eyes were elsewhere. If Barziya wished to assert his right of kingship over the area, he would be forced to defend it. So far, he'd gotten away with not doing so by never stationing soldiers there. Always a coward, he refused to even chance upsetting King Dragonsblood, even if it cost the lives of Arcadians.

As long as word had not yet reached the Bladesworne's of her disgrace, of the king's decree, perhaps Nadia could force them into a rebellion against the king on her behalf. If the king's soldiers skirmished with the berserker clan in the flatlands, whatever disgrace she'd brought upon herself wouldn't matter. Illustrus Bladesworne was already doing his level best to dodge the brutish king's call for warriors. If she gave their family one more reason to rebel, maybe she could do as she'd always planned. And if she succeeded, maybe her family would see her as a good daughter once more.

"Nadia!" Darius bellowed furiously.

But succeeding would mean leaving Darius behind, and cutting out the part of her heart he'd taken up residence in.

She looked back.

A mistake.

Darius' face was darkened by rage and his horse was gaining on hers. Her heart ached.

No, no, if he caught her, if she let him, her fate would be unbearable. *Love leads to ruin.*

She could not accept the life of a mere wife, forever the shadow of a man, no matter who that man was. She could not accept the life of a temple servant, nameless, faceless, powerless—nothing. No matter what she had to do, no matter what blood she needed to shed, she could accept no fate less than that of her greatest ambitions. Anything else would be intolerable. Even if she had to stand alone, with only her magic to aid her, Nadia would have the power of her dreams or she would die trying. She'd already lost her family's loyalty with the king's ire, she'd lost her safety with her flight, she'd lost her heart to a man who should be her enemy. What did it matter if she had to bloody her hands a little more?

What did it matter if she had to break his heart and hers to be free?

"Nadia! Stop!" Darius called, only a few paces from her side.

She pushed her horse harder, but the beast was already running as fast as its legs would carry it.

Darius reached out, trying to snag her reins. She made to hit him with her horsewhip. He flinched away, but the look in his crimson eyes told her he would not be dissuaded. No matter her attempts to deter him, her horse was already slowing and he was riding right next to her. With her next attempt, he grabbed her whip and pulled her sideways. She released her grip on the whip, but not soon enough. Grabbing her by the waist, he unseated her from her horse, dragging her over the saddle of his. Not wishing to be trampled, she was forced to lie across his lap as he slowed their horses to a trot, bringing them back to the margins of the forest.

Ah gods, was her bid for freedom, for her future, already at an end?

When he dismounted, he dragged her off the saddle with him, an unbreakable grip on her shoulders.

"What in the gods unknowable names were you thinking?! The main road was within sight! You could have been spotted! Captured! Killed!

Your horse could have planted a hoof in a ditch and thrown you! Answer me, Nadia!"

"I can't..." her voice wavered. Even now, when she'd run from him, when she'd raised a weapon against him, all he cared for was her safety. She swallowed, her racing heart thundering in her ears. "I can't go to the Temple."

"Why in the hells not?"

"I will never be happy there."

"Nadia..." he sighed, grip slackening as the anger left his eyes. "It won't be so bad. It'll be peaceful, sedate, maybe a bit boring, but we'll have each other and our whole lives ahead of us. No more war, no more politics, no more scheming, no more running for our lives. We won't even have to worry about our shit families. That has to count for something, right?"

"Darius, I..." How did she explain to a man who had always had power what it was to yearn for it, to desire it with her whole being, to know in the darkest parts of her soul that she would always crave it? "I need the politics and the scheming. I need the power to choose my own fate. I need these things like I need to breathe, Darius. I would rather spend the rest of a short life running in the hope that I could have that power than rot in the Temple, or be bound to someone who cannot or will not let me achieve it. I have spent my whole life planning to change the world, and I refuse to give that up."

"Even if it costs you your life?"

"Even then." She sighed. "I am not a good person, Darius. I can never be happy with a simple life. I would never be happy as just a man's obedient wife."

He smiled wryly.

"I could never picture you as obedient."

"Then what *do* you picture, Darius? What is it you want from me?"

"I just..." he paused, eyes sad and voice wistful, "I just want you, Nadia. Whatever else is in the picture is immaterial. You're all that I want."

Her heart leapt to her throat. No, she would not let him win her over with a confession.

"You say that, and yet you know nothing of me. You have no idea what I desire most. You know nothing of the life I had planned for myself. All you know is a pretty face."

Undeterred, he moved closer, a hand at the small of her back.

"Then tell me what you want, what you need, and let me prove to you that I am the only one worthy of giving it to you."

"I want..." Could she really say it out loud? To this man? When she'd never even spoken the words to her own brother, her closest confidant? She pursed her lips. Well, she supposed if nothing else, it would finally make him leave. "I want the power to choose my own fate, to finally know what it is to make choices, instead of being handed them, of being forced to adapt to everyone else's foolish, cruel whims! I want the power to shape the world around me, instead of being forced to bend until I break! I can't have that as a nobilissima, as the wife of an illustrus, not even as a princess or a queen! I want to be an empress. I want all of Lethe to be mine."

"Lethe hasn't been an empire since—"

"Since the very first mage Arcadius claimed Lethe for the rest of us."

A glorious past she would use to unite the disparate kingdoms, it's every symbol mined and refined to suit her agenda. No one could deny it had been a time of wealth, prestige and plenty. And she would recreate it, use it, until the people of Lethe could no longer envision a world, a future, as divided as their present. Until the time before her empire was nothing more than a distasteful memory of hunger, horror and deprivation.

"And how did you plan to go about it? Because unless you've forgotten, we have a pissed off king coming for our heads and a war raging across the continent. We have no allies, no stronghold, no army. Hells, we don't even have more than a single sword between us."

Why did he look like he was considering her wishes, rather than staring at her like she'd sprouted three extra heads? He was by no means pleased, but he wasn't rejecting her either.

"I had plans before your father decided he needed my neck to appease him. I'm working on a back-up." She scowled.

"Then what were your original plans?"

"I had...I had planned to cement marriage alliances in the right places. By taking advantage of whatever bloodshed the war offered, I could kill off the royal families of Lethe after putting my brother and sisters in their courts. The war has weakened them all. This is likely the only chance to change things. The people of Lethe want peace and a good harvest. They care very little who sits on the thrones as long as their needs are met and they can live peacefully. But so long as the kingdoms exist, there can be no lasting peace, even if this war ends. If I were to make Lethe an empire, and I was its empress, I would finally have the power and freedom to reshape Lethe."

"You planned to kill every royal family in Lethe?" He blinked owlishly.

"Yes."

"Even mine?" he asked, his tone suspiciously even.

Even me? His eyes asked the question his lips would not form.

"Yes."

He scowled.

"How?"

Not, 'how could you,' or 'I thought there was more between us,' just 'how.' She supposed she should be grateful for that small mercy.

"Recall that I was going to marry into a large family of berserkers."

"Even berserkers burn."

"Eventually, yes, but the Bladeswornes have been desperate to see combat, which is what I would have offered them. With Phokas' help, we steered my family into an alliance with them. King Firetongue only wanted them as guard dogs." She sighed. "Not that it matters anymore. Without the marriage, it's a moot point."

Darius' eyes were faraway, no doubt contemplating just how foolish she was. He ran his hands over his face in frustration, shooting a longing glance at the Temple in the distance. He sighed. Perhaps he was thinking about leaving her behind. After all, her plans were now useless, yet still they chained her to a life she was unlikely to ever attain.

"Where are the Bladeswornes? I never did find where they ran off to."

It was not what she expected him to say.

"My family's lands in the Flatlands Pass. Strategos Illyia will march on it soon, if my scouts are to be believed. I had hoped to whet their appetite with the battle to come."

She trusted the berserkers would be tempted to fight, given the chance, even if she never made it back. Otherwise the blood of her friends, neighbours and people would water fields of ash.

"You have scouts?"

"I have a great many allies doing me any number of favours, but none of them have any more power than I do." Her network of servants was exceedingly helpful, but not especially powerful—not yet.

"It's the servants, isn't it?" He smiled

"Yes," she grumbled.

"Always did wonder why no one stopped me from getting into the townhouse or from sneaking into your bedroom," he muttered, shaking his head. "Alright, I can see how your plan would work for my family, but why would the other kings fall for it? Who is going to let a clan of berserkers into their homes? How did you plan on getting your family into their courts?"

The hope in her heart struggling to take over was a dangerous thing. She crushed it as mercilessly as was possible. Maybe he only wished to hear the fullness of her schemes in order to talk her out of them. It certainly wasn't so he could talk himself into them.

"Isn't it obvious? The war has raged for six years now. Six years of poor harvests at best. Even the royal stockpiles are getting dangerously low. Famine is widespread everywhere in Lethe except Arcadia and maybe the kingdom of Temenos. I would offer our surpluses and the magic of my family in exchange for marriage alliances. And any such cargo and passengers would need to be jealously guarded on the way to the royal courts."

"Guarded by your berserkers."

"Yes."

"And that would still only work once or twice."

"That would be enough. If even two of the kingdoms were truly united, it would quickly tip the balance of power."

Better still if those kingdoms were Arcadia and Kolkhis, and the most dangerous of the kings, King Dragonsblood, was dealt with first.

The smile that spread on Darius' face was slow and wicked.

"You really are the most cunning woman I've ever met."

"Is that a compliment?" She raised her brows as he pulled her close.

"Yes."

Her cheeks heated as his face was nose to nose with her own.

"Darius..." she said, full of longing and frustration. She gripped the fabric of his tunic, not knowing if she wanted to pull him close or push him away.

"I will give you Lethe, Nadia. I will make you an empress or I will die trying."

She gasped, losing her hold on the hope in her heart.

"How?"

"Well, we have no army or allies. Let's start by getting your berserkers."

"They're not mine. Not anymore."

"Not yet they're not, but they will be."

"You've pretty words and boldness aplenty, I'll grant you, but it means nothing."

She could not let herself get carried away. Nothing had changed, except maybe their immediate destination.

"Is that a challenge?"

She simply glared back.

"Then I'll prove myself to you. But once I have, I expect a suitable reward."

"What reward?"

Her heart raced at the look of pure possessiveness in his ruby gaze.

"You, Nadia. When I've won your berserkers to your cause, then I want you. All of you. I want you to be mine in *every* way. *Forever*."

A shiver stole down her spine at his heated whisper. Whether it was a portent of doom or a sensual promise was something only time would tell.

CHAPTER 9

Some women wanted the romance of poetry, others wanted pretty baubles and the security that only gold could offer. Nadia wanted an empire. Had anyone besides her proposed the scheme, he would have laughed in their face and gone on with his day. Many a king had tried to recreate the founding empire—none had succeeded. Then again, none had tried while Lethe had been weakened by half a decade of war and famine. If ever there were a time when such a gambit could succeed, it was now.

Arcadia was one of the few kingdoms that could boast a position of strength, its people largely unaffected by the war, its harvests uninterrupted. Had his father been the least bit bold, he might have struck out at their weakened neighbours, especially Apollonia, just south of Firetongue Keep. Now Darius was glad that he hadn't, for it gave Nadia's plan a chance to come to fruition—but only if he could convince the berserkers to follow him.

Knowing what he did of the Bladeswornes, they would never have followed Nadia's advice, nor respected her leadership or vision. But they would respect him, even if all he did was speak the same words she had. Even if all he did was act like his father and position himself in their good graces.

"Nadia, before we arrive, we need to talk."

Their horses trotted side by side on a trail adjacent to the main road. Even this far out, they still needed to be cautious of his father's men.

"I'm listening."

"Illustrus Bladesworne and his family will never accept your advice directly. You know that, right?"

She rolled her eyes.

"Of course I know that. Phokas has been my mouthpiece all my life. I shall simply be using you this time."

Did she not believe he could win them over?

"*From now on*, you mean."

"Only if you succeed."

"*When* I succeed."

"Think whatever you like. They've proven to be more stubborn than mules. We spent six months negotiating a marriage, and probably would have spent several more, and that was something they were agreeable to. You'll have your work cut out for you."

That he would, but he knew soldiers, and he knew battle fanatics. Promise them glorious bloodshed and they would at the very least entertain him and his notions.

He waved off her concern.

"What I wanted to talk to you about is how you want to do this in future. If people believe I'm the one with the brilliant schemes, they'll target me. I'd prefer it that way, to be honest. I can defend myself better than you can. We can't keep it under wraps indefinitely that you're the strategist, but I want to be your shield for as long as possible."

And if he died, at least she would live on, and her dreams would have a chance to come true. He was ashamed that he'd never considered that she might want more than the life of a noblewoman. She hadn't been wrong to question him either—the kind of future he'd envisioned was one only he'd desired. Darius would not make the same mistake again.

"I can accept that, but I think we need a more complicated strategy. If you succeed, and we survive the next few weeks, we need to be more than just a warrior king and his smiling wife. I need you to play the part of the implacable tyrant, and I will be your level-headed wife, the only one capable of making you see reason. Our allies and enemies should fear you, and see me as their sole hope of mercy. They will be less inclined to replace me if they know only I hold the leash on your temper. It will make manipulating them simpler for me."

He rubbed his scruffy jaw, grimacing. Gods, he'd never wanted to be anything like his father, but the one thing Barziya did instill was fear. At the very least, he knew exactly how much of a bastard he needed to be.

They cleared the treeline, their horses trotting through fields of golden stalks, bowing in the breeze, heavy with grain. Some distance off, a scattering of simple buildings, with her family home spread wide over the hilltop, the stone walls painted in reds and blues.

"I can work with that." He nodded, doing his best not to scowl. He pushed the unpleasantness from his mind, imagining her as his wife in truth. "Do you really think you can keep your tongue and temper in check? Isn't that like asking you to pretend to be your opposite?"

She looked at him then, her hazel eyes soft and solemn, no hint of chagrin.

"I would be asking the same of you, Darius, at least in public. And for that, I'm sorry. Lethe isn't a place that values my ambition, just like it isn't a place that values your kind heart. Maybe one day, we'll get to see that Lethe. Maybe we'll be the ones to make it so."

His heart blazed with warmth at her words. She truly thought him a good man, one with a kind heart. For a man who had struggled with the fear he would one day become his father, it was the greatest of compliments and the most precious of balms. It soothed a part of his soul he hadn't realized needed tending. If possible, he loved her all the more.

If going through with this mad scheme could bring about such a world, then maybe all the blood they intended to shed on the way would be worthwhile.

Darius relaxed in his seat as one of the servants tidied his unruly beard. Upon their arrival, the household had been whipped into a frenzy of concerned pampering. From their suspicious gazes, they hadn't decided what to make of him yet, but he'd laid the charm on thick, and the Verdant servants were just now opening up in his presence.

"Has Nadia been tended to?" he asked.

"Of course, Your Highness."

"And have the Bladeswornes treated her poorly since she arrived?"

She'd come with him in tow, their days on the road obvious to all, and not a chaperone in sight. It was obvious what they would say, and if there was one thing he'd learned in his short time here, it was that Nadia was treasured by her servants. She had a way of winning people over who were often overlooked by others—an admirable trait.

"In truth, Your Highness, they have been less than kind in some of their comments."

He waited until the blade was no longer near any of his vital points before he banged his hand on the armrest of his chair, his face reddening with all the rage he could muster. The servant flinched.

"Those dogs! I'll have their heads!"

"Your Highness, please calm yourself. The nobilissima would surely be upset if bloodshed were to occur in her home."

"And yet those dogs have abused her hospitality by slandering their host!"

"They do more than slander," grumbled a servant laying out appropriate attire for him.

The servant trimming his beard glared at the man with the change of clothes.

"Tell me more," Darius invited him.

After a tense, angry staring contest between the two servants, the bolder of the two approached him, kneeling.

"They're barely civilized, Your Highness. All they care about is the prospect of violence. They start petty fights in the hopes of those fights escalating, reaching for the pommels of their swords without hesitation. Ever since they've arrived, our household has lived in terror. And now that the nobilissima has returned, I fear they will wreak havoc."

"I will deal with them, fear not. The nobilissima and I are of a mind on this."

"Thank you, Your Highness." The servant bowed his head, shoulders slumping with relief.

The moment he was presentable, he made his way to the atrium where the berserkers sharpened their blades in a huddle. In the open air, the sunlight glinted off their steel weapons, the berserkers' mutinous expressions reflecting in the mosaic-tiled pool at their feet. Fragrant, bright blossoms peeked out of painted vases along the frescoed walls. At least the interlopers took care not to give free reign to their mage gifts—for now. Nadia was already present, her smile strained as she offered them food and drink only to be sneered and leered at. The servants fared no better as they extended their hospitality, only to be rudely rebuffed.

Time to be the brashest, boldest, cockiest man alive.

"Greetings, Bladeswornes." Darius' wink was a shameless insult, given the circumstances.

"Tell us why we should let you live." The biggest of the Bladeswornes stood, his hand hovering over the pommel of his blade. Not even within the house did they go unarmed, crazy bastards. This one was Artemius Bladesworne, if Darius recalled correctly.

"Because if I die, you'll only live to see a few more battles, at most, before you die a dog's death."

The lot of them stood at that, their eyes gleaming with the promise of bloodshed. He'd thought the servants had been exaggerating. Apparently not.

"Is that a threat?" another asked, almost hopefully.

Darius laughed.

"Simple statement of fact. Come, sit. We have much to discuss."

"Like how you've soiled our cousin's fiancée? You come in here acting like you own this estate, so don't pretend you haven't sampled the goods! You spit on the honour of our great house!" Artemius thundered.

Darius squeezed his hands into fists, nails biting into his palms as he got his anger in check. It took all of his restraint not to choke the life out of Artemius for the insult. But these were men hoping for a fight, hoping to provoke him into making the first move. They wanted an emotional response, and he couldn't give it to them.

"If your great house wanted her so badly, they would not have spent the last six months haggling like fishmongers over insignificant details. Let's be frank, shall we, man to man? You were hoping that Strategos Illyia would show up sooner rather than later, to force her family into giving you an inordinate dowry as incentive to protect them."

Unashamed, Artemius scoffed.

"Man to man, you say? And yet is there any greater dishonour to a man than being cuckolded?" Artemius glowered, ignoring Darius' gibe.

"How about dying of old age, weaponless, feeble and weak? Or for that matter, dying in a battle and suffering the Damnatio Memoriae? What honour is there in a battle that no one speaks of, fought by men who have been erased from history?" That seemed to give them pause, their hands lowering from their pommels. He'd finally hit on their true fears. And as a prince, it was one of the many punishments he could bestow. "The nobilissima is my fiancée now, and has requested as proof of our engagement that I slay the strategos on his way here. You are welcome to join in the battle to come, unless you would prefer I reap all the glory for myself."

"No one here cares to help you in your endeavour, boy! We'll return to our lands, now that there is no reason to be here." Artemius lifted his bearded chin with a sneer.

"So you prefer to be guard dogs instead of warriors, instigating petty fights in the hopes they become brawls? My father will be pleased. He's been so eager for you to look menacing at Firetongue Keep, kitted out in spotless mail and frowning at all who enter. You might even make it out of the Great War without ever seeing a single battle. Your wives will be pleased." He raised a brow and smiled, happy to finally see the composure of a few crack. He'd all but called them cowards.

"Watch your tongue! Even princes bleed," Artemius growled.

His heart leapt in his throat. Was now the best time to lay out their plan? His eyes found Nadia, and though it was only a split second, he saw her smile and nod.

"As do kings..." Darius let that statement hang in the air, ripening the longer he remained quiet with a vicious smile on his face. The berserkers looked to each other, excitement like electricity crackling in the room. It wasn't every day open treason was discussed, or even alluded to. Thankfully, the Bladesworne kin were intelligent enough to take his meaning.

"And what glorious battles would you partake in, if you had your way?"

"I would make war with the whole of Lethe, and all who swore fealty to me would fight alongside me. I have no use for ornaments and guard dogs. And I have even less for those too afraid of getting burned to snuff out weak, flickering embers."

A taunt and a promise. These men who cared only for battle, glory and honour were as easy to manipulate as Nadia had assumed, so long as the words came from the lips of another man. Gods, she'd have had the lot of them wrapped around her finger within a week. He was glad that he was her ally and not her enemy—not anymore.

The pounding of footsteps and slamming of doors interrupted whatever the berserkers might have said. Darius cursed. The disruption could not have come at a worse time. He glared at the man who dared disturb them so noisily.

Covered in mud from his feet to his knees, sunburnt and stinking of horse, the man leaned heavily on the nearest pillar, breath sawing in and out.

"The strategos has come early," he wheezed, collapsing. "He'll arrive in the pass in the next hour!"

Perhaps this interruption was not so ill-timed after all. Darius leapt from his seat and strode for the door.

"Get me a horse, a blade and armour." He stared at the berserkers, strung tight as they wavered between avenging the dishonour that was Darius' theft, and the potential for bloodshed. "What say you, Bladeswornes? Will you fight, or will you flee?"

Would they ally themselves to him, or would they submit themselves to his father?

The berserkers followed without a word of protest, kitting themselves out and strapping an inordinate amount of steel to their persons. Mounting up, they raced to meet the enemy in battle. All the while, Darius took the lead position.

Because they hadn't had time to position themselves in advance, Strategos Illyia would know they were coming, the cloud of dust their horses kicked up as plain as a smoke signal of their position. Darius doubted the berserkers would be satisfied with anything less than a full frontal assault. Hopefully Artemius would be the first to die, and would pay for insulting Nadia with his life.

As they neared the strategos' group, some of his worries eased. With the berserkers at his back, Darius was not outnumbered, and his enemies were encumbered with a long line of heavily laden carts—full of looted goods no doubt. It meant that their fighting force was only just beginning to move into position to meet them, the rest straggling in from a distance. The vegetation closest to the main road was sparse, but the trees bordering it were young, the woods not yet thick enough to hide archers or reinforcements. One less thing to worry about.

Darius took out his sword and raced into battle amidst the cries of the berserkers. Most of his ostensible allies leapt from their horses to make the final charge on foot, blades in hand and bloodlust transforming their fierce faces into monstrous visages. Never had he seen such recklessness. Certain they would be trampled down to the last man, he was shocked when instead their blades cleaved through enemy horses and riders alike.

While they were busy enjoying their skirmish, Darius remained atop his horse. Lighting cart after cart on fire, setting panicked horses free, he forced the enemy soldiers to choose between fleeing for their lives, protecting their treasures or recapturing their horses. Either way, they would do so with his flames at their backs.

With the caravan engulfed in flames, he raced back towards the front, cutting down any soldier he passed. Not one had decided to flee. But all who had managed to dodge his blade raced after his horse—right into the steel of the berserkers who had left the main scrum.

By the time he neared the front, only the enemy mages with gifts uniquely suited to battle had managed to hold their own against the berserkers, including Strategos Illyia, a lightning mage. Lost to their frenzy, the berserkers charged into the melee with the strategos, heedless of becoming lightning rods with their steel armour and weapons. Charred, exploded corpses littered the battleground alongside limbless bodies, dead horses and deep crimson pools.

He would need to take the leader by surprise, or else risk becoming a target for lightning himself. Sheathing his sword, Darius spotted the perfect weapon. He grabbed the spear of a fallen berserker, rode past the melee and struck Illyia through the leg. It was enough of a distraction for the nearest berserker to make inroads and lop off the man's head.

Sword in hand once more, Darius turned his horse, taking down any who escaped the ravening berserkers, the lot of them drunk on death and dismemberment. Once the main force was dealt with, they followed him, bright eyed and screaming, as he raced down the line of burning carts, ripping apart every enemy soldier Darius failed to send to a swift death with his own blade as he passed.

When he reached the front of the enemy's smoking caravan, ash choking him as the wind brought the searing heat of the blaze close enough for his horse to shy, he raised his sword and let out a triumphant cry. The berserkers followed suit, raising their blades to the sky before sinking them deep into the earth. No longer holding onto steel, their eyes cleared enough that he was certain they heard him.

"If you fight alongside me, if you swear fealty to me, I swear upon my name you will spend the rest of your lives in glorious battle! You will never be my guard dogs, you will be my vanguard! I will feed you only the most brutal of foes, and you will drink only the bluest of blood! Join me, and we will conquer the whole of Lethe!"

To a man they knelt, hands over their hearts, eyes shining with vicious delight.

"We swear our swords to Prince Darius Firetongue!"

CHAPTER 10

When the first tendrils of smoke had reached above the treeline in the distance, Nadia's heart had seized with worry. As those same tendrils formed a dark cloud, her fears intensified. There was nowhere left to run now, no ally at her side, with a tyrant at her back and a small army before her. She'd risked everything on Darius and the chance the berserkers would be triumphant. As the sun rose high in the sky, a servant burst into her chambers, out of breath.

"The prince and the Bladeswornes have returned victorious, Nobilissima! And they're bringing wagons that look like they're one stiff breeze away from coming apart."

Her feet were moving before her mind caught up. She raced through her family's marble halls, past bucolic scenes painted on the walls, skidding over polished, simple mosaic patterned floors and pushed past ornate doors four times her height. There, down the tree-lined path, was Darius atop his mount, smiling and joking with the most quarrelsome of the berserkers. Throat choked with emotion, her eyes stung, blurring his image. She gripped the wood of the door, so as not to fall to her knees with relief.

When he spotted her standing there, he broke off his conversation and raced towards her, all but vaulting off his horse to sweep her up in his arms. She threw her own arms around his neck, trembling as her heart caught up with what her senses were telling her. Darius was alive.

For a time, they simply revelled in each other's touch. The future was far from certain, but a weight lifted off her chest. In Darius' arms, she felt like she could conquer the world. The Flatlands were safe, the berserkers had allied with Darius, and the future she'd dreamed of was now a possibility.

"Prepare yourself, Nadia. Because tonight, you're mine," he whispered in her ear.

His kiss was hard and swift and left her lips tingling and her mind dizzy. There would be no life in the shadows next to him, no life of unimportance, no life spent being unheard. Gods forgive her, but she wanted him—she wanted the man who looked at her like she was Oblivion's greatest gift, who listened to her every word, and heard her heart's every longing whisper as no other had. Love had not led her to ruin, but to her heart's truest desire.

As he smiled, it took an effort of will to untangle the urgent grip she had on his thick hair. Heart racing, she stared after him as he led his horse and the berserker guests to the stables, directing a long line of wagons reeking of smoke to park. Nadia shook her head. She couldn't be daydreaming at a moment like this. The Bladeswornes would want a feast to celebrate and the kitchens had to be informed.

The rest of her day passed in a blur of frenzied activity. The injured to be tended, baths to be drawn, new clothes to be set out, armour and weapons to be mended and repaired and horses to be cared for came first. Then wagons of plunder needed to be sorted and organized, corpses to be dealt with, wine to be served and a feast to be laid out. It left blessed little time or energy for anxieties. But as the sun set and the stars glittered in the night sky, the celebration died down, and berserkers were carried off to their beds as they passed out. Eventually, lamps were put out and sleepy-eyed servants left to clean up after a long day.

Nadia waited in her rooms, trying to mentally and emotionally prepare herself for Darius' visit. She'd promised herself to him in exchange for his victory today and she was a woman of her word. It wasn't as though she was entirely ignorant—she'd grown up amongst farms after all. Neither was she opposed to intimacy with him. She planned to wed him, such things were expected. She could even admit to herself that she loved him. Yet as her first kiss had taught her, she'd been kept rather ignorant of the finer points all her life. What if it was terrible? What if she hated every moment? What if he was disappointed with her?

By the time he swept into her rooms it was nearly the middle of the night, her bedroom lit by a myriad of flickering oil lamps. He closed her door, silent as a shadow. When he stood in front of her, she was trembling anew, no matter how hard she tried to control it.

"Nadia, are you frightened?" he asked, a calloused hand on her cheek.

"No," she lied.

And yet her next shaky breath betrayed her as his fingers trailed down her arm.

"We don't have to do any of this tonight. We don't have to do anything until you're ready."

There was sincerity in his gaze, and the panicked animal in her began to relax. She placed her hand atop his as his thumb stroked her cheek.

"What if...what if I don't like it?"

"If you don't like something, then we stop, maybe try something different, something you *do* like."

That sounded suspiciously reasonable.

"It's...that simple?"

"Yes."

Surely he didn't mean that.

"And you would stop, if I asked you to? Just like that?"

"Yes, just like that."

His fingers traced soothing patterns on her back and she found herself pressing up against him, drawn to the heat of him, to the gentle promise in his ruby eyes. Maybe he was telling the truth. Maybe it wouldn't be so bad.

"Did you enjoy our kisses, Nadia?"

She nodded, swallowing her trepidation. His kisses had been like strong wine, muddling her mind and inflaming her.

"Say the words," he commanded, soft yet unyielding.

It sent a thrill down her spine.

"Yes, I...I enjoyed kissing you," she stammered, face flaming.

"Do you like it when I touch you?"

The soft glide of his fingers sent another shiver rolling down her spine.

"Yes," she whispered.

"And when I hold you close?"

His hand, hot and sure, pulled her as close as two people could be. It felt, if not what she would term safe, then at the very least highly agreeable.

"...Yes."

"Then we'll start with the things you like. And if you want more, all you have to do is ask."

She bit her lip, eyes askance. Was he teasing her? Darius must know or at least suspect her ignorance. He stilled, sensing her trepidation.

"Tell me what has you frightened."

"It's not fear it's just..." She looked back up into his eyes, fighting the hold her embarrassment had on her tongue. "I don't know what to ask for." If her cheeks were heated before, they were positively flaming now.

"You don't have to know exactly what you want. If you ask for more, I will give you more, and then you can tell me if you like it or not."

She released a pent up breath, and though her heart hammered in her chest, it was no longer out of uncertainty, but anticipation.

"I would like to kiss you, Nadia. Would you like that?"

"Yes."

Their lips met, a soft, gentle brush. His fingers threaded through her hair, anchoring her as he deepened the kiss. As his tongue stroked hers she moaned, gripping the fabric of his tunic in her fists. The kiss ignited a fire in her, melting her shyness, her hesitation. Swept away, she pulled him closer, matching every pleasurable stroke of his tongue. When he broke their kiss, it took all she had to stifle a needy groan.

His heavy-lidded gaze was heated and smug. He waited. Damn him. Darius really was going to make her beg. But her pride was a small thing to discard at that moment, when the prospect of further pleasure awaited.

"More," she breathed.

He obliged, nibbling the lobes of her ears, kissing his way down her neck. New, heady sensations had her panting with need.

"More," she pleaded.

He lowered her gown, baring her breasts. Hands gripping them, his thumb stroked her nipple as his mouth found the other. Her fingers threaded through his hair as she cried out. She must be the greediest of women, because everything he did made her needier.

"More," she whimpered.

He dispatched her gown with ruthless efficiency before stripping out of his own tunic. He crowded her, backing her up until the backs of her legs met the bed. Pushing her down, his smile was pure masculine lust. She wished she'd lit more lamps. Even in the dim, flickering light he was a sight to behold. Wide and thick and strong, no part of him was delicate. His manhood gave her some pause, however. Perhaps it might have been better for her if *one* part of him had been delicate.

"I think you're really going to like this."

But instead of joining her on the bed, he knelt before it, pulling her hips towards his face. The promise in his eyes silenced the protest before it reached her lips. Or maybe it was the confidence with which he bent his head to his task. Whatever the case, she was glad of it. The moment his tongue touched flesh, she was lost once more, riding waves of pleasure that engulfed her, dragged her under, eclipsing everything that had preceded it. When his tongue brought her to unknown heights and pushed her over, she screamed his name, hands gripping his head as her body bucked.

When she came back to her senses, he was grinning. Gods below. At least she needn't fear disliking anything between them.

"More?" he asked.

"Yes."

She thought he might finally join her on the bed, but instead he bent his down and lashed her with his tongue again, one finger, and then two, entering her, stretching her. He drove her to another precipice before ruthlessly throwing her over. Her throat felt raw from her cries, from screaming his name like a prayer, from begging for more.

Only then did he climb atop her in the bed, urging her back onto the plush surface. He took her hand and placed it on his manhood, urging her to stroke it. She'd never imagined how soft it would be, nor how unyielding. The rest of him was so hard and rough, and she delighted in touching him wherever she could. As she learned the shape of him, what made him groan and gasp and growl, there was an ache in her that demanded tending.

"I need something more."

He swallowed, nodding.

"This may hurt a little, but only the first time."

He positioned himself over her and pressed himself to her entrance, sliding in by slow degrees. There was a definite twinge of pain as her body accommodated his. He uttered not a single word of complaint as she dug her nails into his back. When he finally stopped moving, she caught her breath as he caught his.

"You feel so fucking good, Nadia. Are you alright?"

In truth, it was uncomfortable and strange, but part of her still ached. Her greed had not yet been sated.

"I think so. Is this...are we done now?"

"Do you want us to be?"

She moved then. He groaned as if in terrible agony. Her sting of pain had lessened. Perhaps she was a selfish woman for demanding more of him, but so be it.

"No."

"Thank the gods. Wrap your legs around me."

The moment she did, he began pulling out of her. Before she could protest, he pushed back inside. In time they found their rhythm, his thrusts and hers meeting as the ache in her was soothed. Bodies pressed close, holding each other as if they might be torn apart at any moment, his lips found hers. Fully locked into their embrace, he slipped a hand between them and touched her as his tongue had, bringing her over the edge as she gasped his name. Hips bucking wildly, he groaned and collapsed over her. As they recovered, their breaths mingling, his expression turned tender.

"I love you, Nadia. I have loved you since the moment I laid eyes on you. And every moment in your company has only made me love you more."

Her heart ached at his words. How often had she been told that love would ruin her? How many times had she told herself those same words? For years she had learned to close off that part of herself, inured to the reality that she was not to expect something as fleeting as love. She'd shut the lid so tight, only one man had ever heard her heart, even when she'd convinced herself she'd silenced it. And here it was, her secret girlish fantasy—love. She pulled him close, shaking with the realisation that it was not a dream, that she was allowed to take what he offered and never look back.

"I love you too, Darius."

CHAPTER 11

Darius woke with the dawn, Nadia still asleep and cuddled up next to him. He smiled into her silky black tresses, remembering their night together. She'd given him her body but more importantly, she'd given him her love. He'd seen it in the way she'd looked upon him after his confession, had heard her heart in her reply, had felt it in his bones when she shook, afraid the fates might part them. Whatever happened now, wherever life took them, so long as he had her by his side, so long as she loved him, everything would be right with the world.

When she opened her eyes he kissed her forehead and went to fetch some food. The kitchens were only just firing up the stoves, and so he gathered what he could that didn't require cooking. Cured meats, bread, oil, fruits and a bit of wine, and then headed back to enjoy some morning bliss with the woman who would be his wife. As he dreamed of the gown she might wear, and he might divest her of, he pushed through the doors to her chamber to find her brushing her hair and decidedly not naked in their bed.

So be it.

He could fix that.

"You look beautiful, Nadia."

"And that food looks delicious." She winked at him.

"No compliments for your soon-to-be husband?" He frowned.

"I would not want you to get ahead of yourself."

Ah, there was her smile. As he set about placing their meal at a nearby table, grinning like the luckiest of fools all the while, a shadow darkened the window of her chamber.

His heart stuttered in his chest. An armed man, his pale eyes fixed on Nadia. It was a man he recognized—his father's only teleportation mage. Darius took the knife he'd procured and threw it at the intruder, only for it to sail out the window. Nadia shrieked. The man was already upon her, fighting to grab hold of her. Nadia could be anywhere in an instant. She could be dragged before his father and it would take Darius days to get back to her, if there was anything left of her to get back to.

Lunging for the mage, Darius tackled him to the ground. If he could cause great enough pain, the mage might not be able to focus enough to use his gift. And yet as Darius grabbed hold of the man's face, raising it up so he could smash it down onto the floor, the simple white and black mosaic tiles underneath him changed between one blink and the next. Instead of black and white tiles, he smashed the man's head down into the scuffed mosaic of a vine. Though the man was now unconscious, ice cold dread shot through Darius' veins.

Faded frescos and tattered tapestries covered a great hall. The grand pillars were chipped, their red paint faded, and the only piece of furniture that gleamed was a golden throne, one upon which his father sat. Waiting beside the tyrant stood all his brothers—cowards and bootlickers the lot of them. They'd fashioned themselves into whatever it was that ensured they never suffered the wrong end of Father's wrath. And now they threatened Nadia. King Barziya looked at her with a crooked smile. She clung to the back of Darius' robe.

Outnumbered and outmatched, with nary an ally in sight, there was only one thing he could do now to forestall their fate. Though his gut churned, he stood tall, helping Nadia to her feet before pushing her to stand behind him.

"I demand the right to contest the throne through ritual combat."

"You have no right!" Barziya lunged from his seat, glaring daggers as his voice echoed throughout the room. And yet despite his outward fury, Darius had seen a flicker of fear in the old man's ruby eyes. He pressed his advantage.

"I have every right, and certainly more than you did when you killed the previous king."

"You are not yet thirty years of age."

He was prevaricating now. His thirtieth year was but several months away. Darius sneered.

"Are you afraid, Father? Afraid that without my deference or my brothers holding me down, you can't defeat me?"

The king's fists shook as a vein popped out in stark relief at his temple.

"I'll have your tongue for that, boy!"

And yet he hadn't moved a step closer, hadn't stormed down towards him, fists and insults flying as was his custom.

"Then by all means, let's take this outside for all to see."

Would he be a coward, or would the king meet the challenge?

"So be it. Lock that bitch up, and give me your sword." He turned toward Tithaeus, the son nearest his side.

Tithaeus dutifully handed Father his sword and made to step towards Nadia.

"Touch her and my first order as king will be to cut off your gods damned hands. That goes for all of you," Darius growled, glaring at the lot of them.

When Tithaeus hesitated, eyes flicking between Barziya and Darius, Barziya pushed him aside with a snarl and strode towards the training grounds. Darius waited until they had all filed out behind the king before following, refusing to let a single one be at his back.

"Darius, what are you doing?" Nadia hissed at him.

"The only thing I can do."

"If Barziya dies, your brothers will turn on you!"

"Yes, some will, which is why, during the fight, I need you to work your magic. The moment one of them steps out of line, or tries to interfere, you kill them, if I don't get to them first."

"Your father is a coward, but he is also cunning. He will have something up his sleeve to disadvantage you during this fight," she whispered as they neared their destination.

"He will try to attack you if I give him half the chance, I'm certain."

"Gods below." She swallowed.

"Nadia, look at me," he commanded, lifting her chin. "You can do this. I've seen you fight twice before."

"I'm no warrior, Darius, it was a miracle we survived."

"I'm not asking you to be a warrior, I'm asking you to use that wicked mind and your mage gift to stay alive. I know you can do this."

She released a shaky breath and nodded, following him out into the morning sun, hopefully not for the last time.

Only his brothers and a few soldiers who were being trained by the owner of the palace, Illustrus Heraklius Lithos, stood round for the occasion, probably so that Father could do his dirty tricks without anyone of power or importance discovering his cowardice.

Once, the grounds must have been a beautiful space. But the weapons racks had seen better days, as had the weapons and armour. Many of the flowering trees along the perimeter had been cut down. Only the creeping rose vines had managed to hang on, and only because they were nearly impossible to kill.

Both Darius and Barziya stood in the centre of the fighting grounds, hard-packed dirt beneath their feet. Stripping out of their robes and tunics, they left on only their trousers and boots. Barziya snatched the sword from the hand of Tithaeus who now held his clothes, while Darius waited for his own. Barziya sneered, grabbing the small dagger from his ornate belt and tossed it at him. It landed at his feet.

"I am owed a sword," Darius ground out.

"And I was owed a filial son!"

Barziya launched the first assault with a ball of flame directed at Darius' torso. He rolled, grabbing the pitiful dagger and dodging the first blow while narrowly avoiding the sword that came down from above. Barziya kept him rolling and lunging on the ground with a constant wave of flame and swipes of his sword. Sweat dripped down into Darius' eyes as the grounds turned sweltering. It didn't help that he was forced to position himself so as not to allow his father's flames to get near to where Nadia sat on a bench, flanked by his brothers. But she'd kicked off her sandals, her bare feet connecting with the earth, as her magic required. Good girl.

In the next split-second between sword and flame, Darius breathed deep and unleashed a torrent of his own flames from his lips. Though his fire didn't burn hot enough to hurt his father, it would be enough to distract him. Barziya's stance weakened, Darius lunged into the opening, blade ready to sink into his father's heart. But in the moment he'd closed, Barziya had regained his balance, sword swinging to meet Darius' side. Dropping the dagger, Darius reached for Barziya's wrist and squeezed as hard as he could, hard enough to feel bones snapping. The sword clattered onto the ground beside them. Crying out, Barziya brought his free hand up to Darius' face, palm full of fire. He grabbed his father's wrist and twisted, even as the flames seared him.

As they grappled, Darius felt the tide of the battle shifting. When Barziya breathed in to spray his face with an inferno, Darius rammed his head into his father's, stunning him just long enough for Darius to trip the old king and twist his arms behind his back. The king's ribs cracked beneath Darius' weight.

Taking his father's wrists in one hand, Darius gripped his father's hair in his free hand and yanked his head up before pounding it into the dirt again and again, until Barziya's cries were no more. Levering himself off, he grabbed his father's blade and raised it high over the prone, defeated king. As he brought it down, a wave of flame forced him to retreat.

"Father said the first to step into the ring to save him from death would become the heir, so now you'll face me, Darius."

Mardonius, his eldest brother, stepped into the ring, sword in hand, and lunged. His battle cry ended with a wet gurgle as a thorny rose vine shot out of the ground and wrapped itself around his neck, dragging him down to the earth. More vines sprouted as his brother struggled, pulling him from the arena, leaving a trail of blood in the dirt. Mardonius struggled to set the vines alight, but every smoking tendril was replaced by a newer vine. Darius' eyes found Nadia's, and he nodded, heart swelling with pride. As Mardonius' struggles faded and crimson pooled around him, Darius turned his eyes to his remaining brothers.

"Does anyone else wish to profane our ritual combat?"

Finding no other volunteers, Darius marched over to Barziya and steeled his heart. The man who was supposed to raise him, to love him, crawled away from him. Only the faintest whisper in his heart protested at what he had to do. He silenced it. Barziya was nothing more than a pathetic, spiteful tyrant—wholly irredeemable. Darius vowed to himself that he would be a better man—to be nothing like his father.

As Darius raised his sword once more, Barziya choked on bloody spittle and eyed him balefully.

"May your children be as treacherous as you."

Darius brought down the sword over his father's neck, ending Barziya's reign and beginning his own.

CHAPTER 12

It was some weeks before a suitably glamorous royal wedding could be arranged. In that time, two more of Darius' brothers had challenged him and two more funerals had been quietly arranged. Given the stress of their position, the cold politeness with which her family treated her now, and the whirlwind of arranging the event, Nadia hadn't been surprised to miss her monthly courses. But not a week after the wedding, she shot out of bed in the night, lunging for the chamber pot as nausea violently churned her gut. For the next few weeks, the sickness would strike at every hour of the day and night. Her first thought had been poisoning, but the healer had assured her that was not the cause. When her ailment continued, she knew for certain what it was.

Seated on a shaded veranda of Firetongue keep, Nadia soaked in the sights of the bustling, colourful walled city, and the emerald mountains disappearing into the clouds in the distance. Upwind from the city proper, the fresh air did wonders for her nausea. She sipped fruit juices and dared to bite into her breakfast.

Darius sat across from her, frowning. In truth, she'd been worried for him in the first few weeks since he'd taken the crown. Though their ruse had already netted them many gains, it weighed on him to act the part of a tyrant. Being back in his family's home, she knew he could not help but be mired in dark thoughts of his own childhood here, where memories merged with the opulence of gold-tiled mosaics, soaring columns, lifelike sculptures and frescos that all but danced across the walls. Perhaps one day her soft-hearted husband would truly hear her reassurances and see what she herself saw—that nothing could ever make him into a monster.

"Nadia, you need to see a healer. You've been sick for weeks now. What if someone is poisoning you?"

"It's not poison, my love."

"Then you've seen a healer already?"

She nodded. She'd had her suspicions confirmed just yesterday.

"Well?"

"I'm pregnant." Nadia smiled.

Darius looked like he'd seen a ghost. Her heart ached for him. She knew exactly what fears plagued him.

"We're going to have a child?"

"Yes, if we're lucky." She placed a hand on her belly. It was early yet and so much could happen.

"I'm going to be a father?"

She smiled. He put his head in his hands.

"What if...what if I become just like him, Nadia?"

Nadia went to Darius' side and held him close, his head cushioned by her chest. He wrapped his arms around her.

"You will never be like your father, Darius. Never."

"How can you know that?" he asked, voice barely above a whisper.

"Because I know your heart. I know the love you are capable of, and I know you will love our child as much as you love me." Hope shone from his ruby eyes, a hope she would nurture for the rest of her days if he let her. She leaned down to kiss him. Before he could pull her in for another, distract her from this conversation, she pulled away, his face in her hands. "Neither of us had the parents we wished we had, but this is our chance to be the parents we always dreamed of having. I know you don't believe me, not yet, but I have every faith you'll be the most indulgent father who ever existed. This is our child, Darius—our family. So long as we love each other, we can meet every challenge."

He pouted, taking her hand and kissing her palm. Darius was not wholly convinced, but one day he would be.

"Why must you always be right about things?"

Ah, her flatterer had returned. Nadia would let him get away with it just this once. She smiled.

"You wouldn't want me any other way."

He grinned then, the darkness banished from his eyes. It would return, she knew, but that just meant she would help him beat it back.

"So, how much would we need to accelerate our plans if we want our child to be born into a peaceful empire?"

She giggled as he pulled her onto his lap. He really did know the way to her heart.

"Oh, my love, I thought you'd never ask."

I hope you've enjoyed Nadia and Darius' story! Want to know how their children shape the fate of Lethe? Check out Poisoned Empire, where a dutiful prince trying to stop a treasonous plot gets entangled with a cynical poison mage: https://books2read.com/pe

If you can't get enough of epic fantasy romance, check out my other books here: https://www.elysethomson.com/#books

Afterword

From the bottom of my heart, thank you for coming on this journey with me. The Firetongue Heir was not a story I imagined writing, but I'm glad I did. I hope it has given you a few hours of escapist fun.

As you may or may not know, reviews are the lifeblood of every author, especially those just starting out. If you could leave a review of *The Firetongue Heir* on Goodreads and retailer sites, that would really help me out!

If you're looking for more epic fantasy romance, check out my other books here: https://www.elysethomson.com/#books

ACKNOWLEDGEMENTS

No book is made without the love and support of a great many people. The Firetongue Heir was no different. I have so many people to thank. Paulina, for helping me iron out the kinks. Alex, for being my rock through the whole process. My family; Mom, Dad, Sylvia, Ross, Kyle, Garrett and Jen for never doubting me. The best writing friends a girl could have (with a group name so lackluster, it doesn't bear repeating) Sophia, Rachel, Asha, Rebecca and Shirley. You kept me sane and gave me a place to belong. My life is richer for having known all of you. And finally, my friends in Pitch'n'Bitch, you always make me smile.

Special thanks to my amazing editor, Sylvia Lovegrin, my talented map maker Alec McKinley, my lovely cover designer and project manager Kostya Biletskiy and Carin, and my dedicated beta reader, Paulina Escudero.

ABOUT THE AUTHOR

Elyse Thomson is the pen-name of an author, bookbinder and self-proclaimed hermit residing in Canada's capital. She writes escapist romantic fantasy with daring heroines, magical mayhem, swoon-worthy romance and court intrigue. Having graduated from University of Toronto with a Bachelors in History and Classics, she is delighted to bring her love of all things ancient to her work. When not writing, she's restoring antiquarian books for a select group of clients, gaming, or snuggling up with either her husband or her neurotic terrier, Freya.

Also By

Mages of Oblivion Series
The Firetongue Heir
Poisoned Empire
Conspirators' Kingdom
Isles of Corruption

Cycle of Calamity Series
The Starlight Princess
The Oracle of Dusk
The Midnight King
...and more to come.

Book Links